RENDEZVOUS

Other books by Melody Carlson:

ON THE RUNWAY SERIES

Premiere (Book One)
Catwalk (Book Two)
Rendezvous (Book Three)
Spotlight (Book Four)
Glamour (Book Five)
Ciao (Book Six)

CARTER HOUSE GIRLS SERIES

Mixed Bags (Book One)
Stealing Bradford (Book Two)
Homecoming Queen (Book Three)
Viva Vermont! (Book Four)
Lost in Las Vegas (Book Five)
New York Debut (Book Six)
Spring Breakdown (Book Seven)
Last Dance (Book Eight)

BOOKS FOR TEENS

The Secret Life of Samantha McGregor series
Diary of a Teenage Girl series
TrueColors series
Notes from a Spinning Planet series
Degrees series
Piercing Proverbs
By Design series

WOMEN'S FICTION

These Boots Weren't Made for Walking
On This Day
An Irish Christmas
The Christmas Bus
Crystal Lies
Finding Alice
Three Days

RENDEZVOUS
ON THE RUNWAY

· ·

BESTSELLING AUTHOR
Melody Carlson

· ·

BOOK THREE

ZONDERVAN

Rendezvous
Copyright © 2010 by Melody Carlson

This title is also available as a Zondervan ebook.
Visit www.zondervan.com/ebooks.

Requests for information should be addressed to:
Zondervan, 3900 *Sparks Dr. SE, Grand Rapids, Michigan* 49546

This edition: ISBN 978-0-310-74861-8

Library of Congress Cataloging-in-Publication Data

Carlson, Melody.
    Rendezvous / Melody Carlson.
        p.   cm. — (On the runway ; bk. 3)
      Summary: Paige and Erin Forrester take their fashion-focused
reality television show to Paris, visiting renowned salons, designers, and
international models, but when they travel to a friend's family estate in
southern France, romance, jealousy, and some surprises threaten the
stability of "On the Runway."
      ISBN 978-0-310-71788-1 (softcover)
      [1. Reality television programs — Fiction. 2. Television — Production
and direction — Fiction. 3. Fashion — Fiction. 4. Sisters — Fiction. 5. Paris
(France) — Fiction. 6. France — Fiction. 7. Christian life — Fiction.] I. Title.
PZ7.C216637Re 2010
    [Fic] — dc22   2010008988

Cover design: Jeff Gifford
Cover photo: Dan Davis Photography
*Interior design & composition: Patrice Sheridan, Carlos Eluterio Estrada &
Tina Henderson*

Printed in the United States of America

14 15 16 17 18 19 20 /QG/ 19 18 17 16 15 14 13 12 11 10 9 8 7 6 5 4 3 2 1

RENDEZVOUS

RENDEZVOUS

Chapter

1

"Not another French movie," *I complain* when I see Paige setting a new DVD on the counter. "We don't want to OD on Paris before we even get there."

"This movie happens to be for Mom. She mentioned that *To Catch a Thief* is one of her favorites, and since she doesn't get to go with us, I thought we could at least humor her a bit." Paige proudly holds up what I'm guessing is a new handbag. "And this, little sister, is a gift from *Hermès, Paris.*"

"A gift or a bribe?" I question as I study the square leather purse with a silver clasp. If it wasn't pink, I might actually like it.

"Let's call it an *enticement.*" She makes a sly grin. "Not that I needed any, since I already wanted to visit Hermès. They're at the top of my list. I absolutely adore Hermès."

"You and Paris Hilton—maybe you were twins separated at birth," I tease. I know the Paris Hilton connection drives Paige nuts. Especially since some celeb-trackers have compared Paige to the hotel heiress, which I personally think is rather insulting to my sister. In my opinion, Paige has more class than Paris. Not that I would ever admit that to anyone.

"For your information, Paris Hilton wasn't the first celebrity to discover Hermès." Paige opens the pink bag, retrieving a black and white scarf, which I assume is also Hermès. "In fact, Jackie O and Grace Kelly were both fans of Hermès decades ago. Hence the *Kelly bag*."

"Kelly bag?"

She holds up her bag and gives me a *duh* expression. "*The Kelly bag.* Designed for Grace Kelly back in the forties, I think. Anyway, it was a long time ago." Paige gets a faraway look. "What I *really* want is the Birkin bag."

"Birkin bag?" I ask, at the risk of a long fashion lecture.

"Jane Birkin, the actress, you know."

"Right." I nod. Of course I know who Jane Birkin is. I *was* in film school back in BS. BS is not what it sounds like — it's actually my new personal shorthand code for Before (the) Show. Anyway, I do know that Jane Birkin was in films during the sixties and later, and I also know she was a fashionista too. Sort of like Audrey Hepburn, but not nearly as popular. "So Jane Birkin has an Hermès bag named after her too?"

"Only the most popular, most expensive, and hardest-to-get handbag of all time." She shakes her head sadly. "The waiting list is, like, years."

"Even for you?"

Paige gives me a slightly catty smile. "I suppose we'll find that out in Paris next week."

"Maybe you'll totally wow Monsieur Hermès and he'll design a special *Paige bag* just for you."

She laughs. "For starters, there is no Monsieur Hermès. Not as in a designer like Calvin Klein or Ralph Lauren. Hermès was originally a family-owned leather company. They made saddles in the 1800s."

"From horses to handbags," I say with irony. "Fashion is so fickle."

Paige places a finger under her chin as if thinking. "Come to think of it, there is a Monsieur Damas-Hermès, but I don't think he's a designer per se. He just runs the company. And he's one of the richest men in the world."

"Will we meet him?" I'm not sure I even care, since I'm not that into money, but it might be interesting.

"I doubt it." She picks up the DVD. "So anyway, back to tonight's plans … I thought we'd do something special for Mom, since it's only three days until we leave for Paris, and I could tell she was feeling bummed last night when we watched *An American in Paris*."

"I thought it was because Grandpa had always been a Leslie Caron fan."

"That's what she wanted us to think," Paige replies. "Really, she wishes she could go with us. She even tried to get time off from Channel Five, but there's no way."

"Too bad she didn't take Helen Hudson up on the offer to help produce the show back when she had the chance last December."

Paige shakes her head. "No way. I would not want Mom producing for us. I love her, but I don't want to work for her. Besides, she's as fashion-challenged as you are."

"Thanks a lot." I make a face at her.

"At least you're learning, Erin. Not that Mom couldn't catch on, but she loves her news job. And what about Fran? She totally gets the show. Can you imagine Mom and Fran working together?"

I nod, knowing that she's right. "So what are you going to do that's so special tonight? I mean, besides the movie."

"I ordered dinner from Patina and I thought we'd set a really pretty table and do candles and flowers—the works. Then we can watch *To Catch a Thief.*" She frowns. "Although I'd rather watch *Funny Face* again. That's such a great Paris movie."

"You mean because it's all about fashion?"

She sighs. "Fashion and Paris and Audrey Hepburn ... it doesn't get much better, does it?"

I chuckle. "Well, I'll admit that I did like *Funny Face*, but that had more to do with the photography focus and Fred Astaire's dancing skills. Plus the fact that Audrey's character was more into philosophy than fashion. I could appreciate her reluctance to become a model."

Paige points her finger at me. "Come to think of it, her character was a lot like you."

"As a matter of fact she was, at least in the first part of the movie. I could sort of relate to her."

"And you know ..." Paige squints at me as she makes a frame with her thumbs and forefingers. "You even kind of look like her."

"Oh, yeah, sure." I shake my head.

"Seriously, Erin, you really do. You're both petite and you both have that pixie sort of face, big expressive eyes, dark hair."

Now I just laugh. "Okay," I say cautiously, "what do you want from me?"

She makes a face. "I'm serious, Erin. You are an Audrey type. I can't believe I never noticed it before. That explains why you look so great in those little black dresses." She frowns. "But maybe we should change your hair. Then you'd really look like her."

"I don't think so."

She takes my chin in her hand, tilting it up. "Really, I'm surprised I didn't see it before, Erin."

"Well, thanks," I say quickly. "I think. But you have to admit that I'm not nearly as skinny as Audrey was. Do you think she was anorexic?"

Paige considers this. "I don't really know for sure, although she nearly starved during World War Two and that probably took its toll. I've always adored Audrey Hepburn, and she was and is the most fashionable woman ever, and every single thing she wore instantly became *haute couture*. That might not have happened if she hadn't been so thin."

"And see—" I point my finger at her. "That's one thing about fashion that makes me want to scream and pull my hair out. *Stick-thin models.* Seriously, if we interview any stick girls in Paris, I might not be able to control myself from asking them about their health and eating habits." I kind of chuckle. "Or maybe I'll just bring in a bunch of croissants and pastries and sit there and noisily pig out in front of them."

Paige presses her lips together with a slightly creased brow. "You know, Erin, that's an interesting angle. The skinny trend had really been changing a couple years ago. Several designers even banned overly thin models from their runways. Now that I think about it, though, it seems like some of them went back to their old ways. Especially internationally. You know, maybe we should do a show that specifically addresses this issue."

"Seriously?"

She nods eagerly as she picks up her cell phone. "I'm going to call Fran right now and see what she thinks."

"What about dinner for Mom? Is there something I can do to help?"

"You could run out and get some flowers. Something Parisian-looking, like you picked it up from a street vendor, okay?"

"What about Jon?" I ask. Jon and Mom have only been engaged for a couple of months, but already he feels like family.

"Don't worry. I already invited him. He even offered to pick up dinner on his way over. We're aiming to eat at eight. Is that okay?" She's got the phone to her ear now.

"Sure."

As Paige begins explaining to Fran about my anorexic models story idea, even giving me credit for thinking of this angle, I grab my bag and head down to my Jeep, trying to remember where the closest florist shop is located. The only one I can think of is a few miles down the freeway and it's commuter traffic time now. Still, it's the least I can do, considering Paige has already put this Parisian dinner plan together for Mom. I'm impressed that she cared enough to go to this trouble. My sister used to be a lot more self-centered and selfish. But I can tell she's changing. And that's pretty cool.

It hasn't always been easy being Paige Forrester's little sister. It's even harder playing Camera Girl, Fashion Flop, or even Jiminy Cricket, as our producer, Helen Hudson, likes to call me, since a big part of my job is keeping Paige out of trouble. But sometimes it can be kind of fun, and I am actually looking forward to Paris.

Yet, at the same time, I wonder just how needed I'll be on our reality show now. Because, to everyone's surprise, Paige has really grown up a lot in the past couple months. She's taking life more seriously, taking responsibility for more things both at work and at home, and actually thinking about others. I realize it's greatly due to Mia Renwick's tragic death on Oscar night.

Talk about a tough wake-up call for everyone. For a few horrid hours, we actually thought it was Paige who'd been killed in the car wreck. That's a night I never want to relive.

Paige had gone to a party with Benjamin after the Oscars, but when they were leaving and she found out he'd been drinking, she refused to ride with him and called a cab. Then Mia made the fatal mistake of getting into Benjamin's car. Now Benjamin has been charged with vehicular homicide but, according to Benjamin, both he and Mia had been drinking. He claims Mia actually caused the accident when she lost her temper and physically laid into him while he was driving in the Hollywood hills, even grabbing and twisting the wheel right before the accident occurred. According to Paige, Benjamin says that Mia was still enraged over their breakup several weeks earlier. Apparently the evidence is starting to support Benjamin's side of the story too, because witnesses reported Mia was acting hostile when she and Ben left together, and her blood-alcohol level in the toxicology reports was very high. Ben's blood alcohol, however, was under the legal limit when the police arrived and administered the Breathalyzer. Also, according to Paige, the police said the skid marks at the scene of the accident match his story—it appears someone changed the direction of the vehicle very suddenly.

Even so, I still think Benjamin's guilty. I realize I'm probably more judgmental than most when it comes to drinking and driving, but I think anyone who gets behind the wheel after consuming alcohol should be locked up for awhile. Really, what could it hurt?

And I'm not sorry that Paige is keeping her distance from Benjamin now. Oh, she talks to him on the phone sometimes. I call them mercy chats. Mostly she's worried that he's feeling depressed. Hey, he should be depressed. A young woman is dead because of him. He can claim it's Mia's fault, but he was the one driving that night. It's not like I hate him or anything. I really don't. In fact, I pray for him every day. I just don't think he should get off too easily. That's all I'm saying.

Thinking all this, and because I'm stuck in traffic that's not budging an inch, I decide to give Blake a quick call, since I know he met with Benjamin this morning. They've actually been doing a Bible study together. I'm not sure if Benjamin is taking it seriously or just hopes that it will improve his bad-boy image, but it sure won't hurt him to hear some truth either.

"Old Ben was pretty bummed today," Blake tells me. "Mia's parents have launched what feels like a full-blown smear campaign. They're talking to publicists and any press that will listen, trying to make Benjamin out to be a murderer who's about to get off scot-free."

"That's not so far from the truth."

"But Erin, they're even comparing him to OJ Simpson. It's like they want him ruined forever. It might even crush his movie deal."

I feel my fingers tightening on the steering wheel, which is pointless since the car isn't even moving. I let go and take in a deep breath. "Okay, I'll admit the OJ thing seems harsh. But it's true that some celebrities beat the rap simply because of their names. It irks me when I see one going off on his merry way like, no big deal. That's just not fair. Maybe losing the movie deal is for the best."

"What about what Jesus said about not throwing stones?" he asks me.

I consider this. "Yeah, I know ... and you're right. But I still think Benjamin should assume some blame for—"

"He knows that he's partly to blame and he wants to admit it. But his attorney is counseling him to continue proclaiming his innocence."

"See, and that bugs me. Maybe if Benjamin took some responsibility for the accident, Mia's parents would let up on him."

"Maybe ..." Blake sounds discouraged.

"I'm sorry, Blake, I don't mean to get on my soapbox. Sorry I sound so negative. I know it's not fair for me to take it out on poor Ben. I really do feel sorry for him and it's cool that you're spending time with him." I peer down the freeway with four lanes of immobile traffic as far as I can see. "It doesn't help that I'm stuck on I–5, and you know how aggravated I get. Patience is not my strong suit."

"Where you headed anyway?"

"I was supposed to pick up some flowers for my mom. Paige is giving her an authentic Parisian dinner tonight."

He laughs. "To make up for leaving her home?"

"Yeah, and we have to watch *To Catch a Thief* with her too, since it's a film that's set on the Mediterranean."

"Man, how many French movies have you girls watched already?"

"Too many." To pass the time, I actually start to list the films. "I really liked *Amelie*," I admit. "And *La Vie en Rose* was amazing, but it was kind of a downer too. Paige's all-time favorite is still *Funny Face*. And any other film with her favorite fashion icon—Ms. Hepburn. We watched *Charade* and even *Sabrina*, which is only partially set in Paris." I notice some of the brake lights flashing and I realize that cars are starting to move. "I better hang up," I say quickly. "Thanks for keeping me company in the traffic jam. Please don't take what I said about Benjamin too seriously. I really do care about him."

"I know you do. And if it's any comfort, I agree with a lot of what you said. But Benjamin needs friends more than accusers right now."

"I'll keep that in mind." I say good-bye and hang up as I put the Jeep into gear. After snarking and going on about DUIs, I'm fully aware that driving while talking or texting on the phone or while doing a lot of other distracting things, like eating, is just as dangerous as driving while intoxicated. After all, I've given Paige that same lecture more than once when I've caught her putting on mascara or lip gloss while she's driving. Although I'll admit I haven't noticed her doing it lately.

Once again I'm reminded that my role on our show might be more expendable than I realized. It might be written out even sooner than I expected. Perhaps it's right around the corner. Because I'm fully aware that *On the Runway* does not need Camera Girl to make it a success—Paige Forrester is what makes the show so popular. Sometimes, like right now, I worry that I'm just an unnecessary distraction. Extra baggage. Another expense. Really, the show would be perfectly fine without me.

And here's what's really weird, especially when I remember how much I whined about being hijacked into reality TV back in the beginning. The truth is that *I would not be perfectly fine without the show.* I really like being part of it. I'm actually learning a lot about film and production—much more than I ever would've learned by now in film classes. And I love being with Paige. I don't even mind being called Camera Girl or Jiminy Cricket that much. What I do mind is not being needed anymore. That seriously worries me.

Chapter

2

"What a delightful surprise," *Mom says as* we sit down to our Parisian dinner. "You girls are so thoughtful."

"It was Paige's idea," I admit. "She's the one who put this all together."

"You got the flowers," Paige reminds me.

"That doesn't quite compare to the Hermès scarf," I point out.

"Well, it's all lovely." Mom sighs as she touches the black and white silk scarf that Paige put around her neck. "It almost makes up for not going to Paris with you girls."

Jon reaches for her hand. "Maybe we'll go there together someday, Brynn."

Mom brightens. "Yes, maybe we will."

The four of us make small talk throughout dinner, but the table feels slightly quiet and I can't help comparing tonight's dinner with ones in the past when Benjamin and Blake have been here. Not that I particularly want to see Benjamin, but I must admit he does make interesting dinner conversation.

When Paige puts in the movie, I offer to be the cleanup

crew. As I clear the table and fill the dishwasher, I catch glimpses of the movie, which is actually pretty funny. Then the phone rings in the kitchen and, not wanting it to interrupt Mom's movie, I quickly answer it. To my surprise, it's my old friend Lionel Stevens.

"Am I interrupting anything?" he asks me.

"No." I move deeper into the kitchen so that the movie-watchers can't hear me. "Just cleaning up after dinner."

"I tried your cell phone and it seemed to be on voicemail, so I thought I'd try your home phone. I actually wondered if you and Paige might be off doing a show somewhere."

I fill him in on our upcoming Paris trip, but as I speak, I'm wondering why he called. Ever since I started doing more things with Blake, Lionel has treated me almost like a stranger. At first it hurt my feelings, then I realized that it might've been his way of showing me that I'd hurt him too. I guess that's just a hazard of being good friends with the opposite sex.

"So . . . you're probably curious about why I'm calling . . ."

"Yeah, I am. I mean, it's been awhile."

"Well, I'm not sure if you and Blake are in an exclusive sort of relationship and—"

"No," I say quickly. "It's nothing like that. Mostly we're just good friends." Okay, that might be a bit of an understatement. But the truth is we're not *that* serious. Although Blake has really been there for me these past few months, I still have a slight reservation when I remember how he broke my heart a year ago.

"So, anyway, I have tickets to a premiere tomorrow night. It's Andy Dresden's film, the one about—"

"The film that's set in Nepal?" I ask eagerly. Lionel and I assisted him in some of the editing to earn extra credit for a film class.

"Yeah. It's called *Edge* and it's supposed to be pretty good. It even won an award last month."

"I'd love to go!"

"Great." Lionel's voice lightens. "How about if I pick you up around seven thirty. Well, unless you'd like to grab a bite to eat first. It might be fun to catch up a little."

"That does sound like fun," I tell him. "I'd love to hear what you've been up to."

"Then, let's say around six thirty."

"It's a deal." Okay, I know that sounds lame, but I almost said *it's a date* then stopped myself. I'm not even sure why I didn't want to say it was a date. I guess I feel slightly guilty about Blake now. Although, to be fair, I've made it pretty clear to him that we're not actually a couple. Not yet anyway ... and, who knows, maybe never. And I really do want to see Andy Dresden's film. But, just to be on the safe side, I decide to gently let Blake know what's up. It seems the right and mature thing to do.

So I finish in the kitchen then go to my room to call Blake. "How'd the French dinner go?" he asks.

"It was pretty good," I tell him. "Mom really liked it. They're watching the movie now."

"But you're not?"

"I'm taking a break."

"To call me?" he says happily.

"Yeah ... well, Lionel Stevens just called me, and he invited me to go to a premiere with him. It's this film that's set in Nepal that a friend of ours produced and Lionel and I did some editing on it last fall and it won some international award and anyway I told Lionel I'd go." This pours out of my mouth all at once, and probably sounds a bit uneasy, which for some reason I am.

"Oh . . . ?"

"And, I don't know, I just wanted to let you know."

"Uh-huh. When is the premiere?"

"Tomorrow night."

"Oh, all right." His tone becomes kind of disinterested and suddenly I feel totally lame for calling. Like why did I think I needed to inform Blake? I don't need his permission to attend a premiere. It's not like we're a real couple. I must sound like an idiot. But the truth is I'm not used to this. This is the kind of problem Paige usually has. Last year I felt like such a reject — Blake's reject. I honestly thought no guy would ever be interested in me again. And now there are *two*?

"So anyway," I say quickly, "I wanted to let you know. I should get back to the movie now." We both say an awkward good-bye and I wonder: Am I imagining things, or did I just make a total fool of myself? I try not to think about that as I watch the second half of *To Catch a Thief* with Mom and Paige and Jon. And that ends up being easier than I thought it would be. In fact, I'm surprised that the movie is kind of interesting, in an Alfred Hitchcock retro sort of way.

Then, as Cary Grant and Grace Kelly are bantering back and forth in a convertible, I can't help glancing over at my sister then back to the screen. Finally, I can't stand it — I have to say something.

"Mom," I begin quietly, "do you think Grace Kelly looks like anyone we know?"

Mom chuckles. "I didn't want to mention it, but yes."

Jon nods. "I can see it too."

"Who do you mean?" Paige asks, oblivious.

I roll my eyes at her.

Paige looks suspiciously at us. "You guys think she looks like *me*?"

Mom makes an innocent shrug and Jon just grins.

"There's a slight resemblance," I say nonchalantly. Now, this is a total understatement. I grab the remote and put the movie on pause, leaving Grace Kelly looking over her shoulder, with her pink scarf frozen in the wind.

"We don't want you getting a big head, Paige," Mom says in a teasing tone. "But, yes, Erin's right. There's a striking resemblance."

"There really is," Jon agrees. "It's no wonder the camera loves you."

Paige leans closer to the TV, studying the frozen shot of Grace Kelly and a slow smile creeps onto her face. "Wow, thanks, you guys. Grace is so beautiful. That *is* a compliment." She throws her head back and laughs. "And, hey, I even have the Kelly bag too."

"So maybe you should cut your hair to look more like hers," I suggest. Okay, I'm teasing now, probably to get back at her for suggesting I change my hair to look like Audrey Hepburn.

"You know, that's not a bad idea." She grins at me. "I will if you will."

"Yeah, right." I toss her a skeptical look.

"Why should Erin cut her hair?" Mom asks. "I like her in a bob."

Then Paige launches into how much I look like Audrey Hepburn and how I should wear the Sabrina haircut, which is extremely short.

Jon looks closely at me. "You know, she's right, Erin, you do look a little like Audrey Hepburn. Too bad you're so camera shy."

I pick up a throw pillow and toss it at him. "I'm not shy around cameras," I challenge him. "As long as I'm behind them."

Mom gets a slightly worried look. "Suddenly I'm feeling a little anxious about having Audrey Hepburn and Grace Kelly strolling around Paris together. What if the paparazzi goes crazy or someone tries to kidnap you two gorgeous girls?"

Paige and I just laugh, assuring her that we'll be perfectly fine. Then, before Mom gets any more concerns about abductions, I turn the movie back on.

"You look nice." Paige gives me a quick head to toe when I finally emerge from my room. I'm wearing about the fifth outfit I've tried on in the last hour. I'm not even sure why I'm being so finicky about my appearance tonight. I tell myself it has more to do with attending the premiere than trying to impress Lionel. At least I hope so.

"Thanks." I look down at the rather simple dress, a Michael Kors "little black dress" that I scored in New York. An Audrey Hepburn style, although I hope Paige won't mention this.

"You still need a little accessorizing," she says with a scrutinizing look. "Those sandals are all wrong for that dress. You need something more classic. Where are you going, anyway?"

I give her a quick lowdown on the premiere as I follow her into her room and kick off my shoes.

"Sounds like fun. And since it's a premiere, you definitely need different shoes." She pulls out a pair of red sling-back pumps and holds them out. "These are a little too small for me. I was going to give them to you anyway."

I can tell by the red soles that they're Christian Louboutin. "Thanks!"

"And you say the movie's set in Nepal," she says as she digs through her closet. "I have the perfect pashmina."

I've barely slipped on the shoes and Paige is wrapping a red paisley shawl around my shoulders. "Voila!" She steps back, nodding in approval.

"Thanks." I finger the delicate fabric. "This is nice."

"Now switch out those earrings for some silver hoops and slip on a silver cuff bracelet and Blake will be fighting the guys off—"

"I'm not going with Blake."

Paige's blue eyes get bigger. "Why not?"

"Because I'm going with Lionel."

"Lionel?" She frowns. "What about Blake?"

"I told Blake about it."

"But I thought you and Blake were—"

"Good friends," I finish for her.

"How does Blake feel about this?"

I kind of laugh. "I don't think he's too concerned."

"Don't be too sure."

"Well, anyway, Lionel and I worked together on this film last fall and I'd really like to see it."

She just nods, but I can tell by her eyes that she's still concerned.

"I really don't think Blake cares," I assure her. "He sounded totally fine."

Paige smiles. "I'm sure you know what you're doing, Erin."

I shrug. "I hope so. Mostly, I just want to see this film." Just then I hear the doorbell ring.

"Have fun," she calls as I head out.

I greet Lionel, and as we go down the stairs, I notice that his hair's a bit longer, cool in an artsy sort of way, and he's going for a retro look with a fifties-style jacket. "I like your fedora," I tell him. "Nice look."

Lionel's smile grows as he pauses on the walkway to check me out better. "You look awesome, Erin."

"Thanks to Paige," I say lightly. "My live-in fashion consultant."

"She's really good at that."

"She's a pro."

"When your show first started, I was a little skeptical," he admits as we cross the parking lot. "I thought it was going to be total fluff."

I laugh as he opens the passenger door of his car for me. "You mean it's not?"

He smiles. "It's not as fluffy as I expected. In fact, I've been enjoying it."

"Seriously?" I feel caught off guard.

He nods and closes the door. As he walks around to the other side, I try to take all this in. First of all, I can't believe the way he's treating me — like this is a real date. And equally surprising is that Mr. No Nonsense Lionel Stevens not only watches our show, he sort of likes it. Very surprising indeed.

"Andy invited me to be on the film crew for another project this summer," Lionel tells me as he drives. "Not as exotic as *Edge*. But it sounds interesting. Kind of a historic documentary that will be shot in Idaho."

"Are you going to do it?"

"Absolutely." Lionel nods.

A small wave of envy rushes over me. "Man, I wish I could do something like that."

Lionel laughs.

"What's so funny?"

"Well, I'm sure a lot of people wish they were doing what you're doing, Erin. Maybe it's just that old 'grass is greener' sort of thing."

"Maybe. But doing a reality show about fashion doesn't seem to compare to shooting a documentary in Idaho."

"Hey, your show will look great on your résumé, Erin. Don't kid yourself."

"You're probably right. I just need to remind myself that it's only the beginning. There'll be plenty of time to do film projects that interest me more in the future."

"And think about the traveling you're getting to do," he reminds me. "Paris next week. London after that. You know how many people would kill for a job like that?"

I nod. "Sorry. I didn't mean to sound like I was complaining. I'm happy for you that you get to work with Andy on a documentary."

"And tonight's film is going to be at Cannes," he says.

"Cool. I know the Cannes Festival is in the spring, but probably not while I'm over there."

"It's not until May."

"Maybe we'll be in London then."

"Maybe you can pop over," Lionel says lightly. "You know, hop a ferry or go in the Chunnel."

I laugh. "Who knows."

It turns out Lionel has picked out an Indian restaurant for tonight's dinner, which is appropriate, since the movie we're going to see is set in that part of the globe. As soon as we are seated, I'm realizing that Lionel isn't quite how I'd been remembering him. For some reason I'd been thinking he was kind of an old stick-in-the-mud, probably because he sort of hurt my feelings when he first heard about our TV show. He acted like it was going to be just another trashy reality show. Now he actually seems to appreciate it. Still, I honestly doubt he'd be watching it if I wasn't part of it.

"I really liked those segments you did on environmentally conscious fashion designers," he tells me after we've placed our orders. "Kudos to you, Erin."

"Thanks!"

As we eat paneer and kofta and baigan, we talk about some recent indie movies and how things are progressing at film school. It almost seems like we're in the same comfortable place where we'd been last fall. I must admit it's rather nice.

"So . . ." he begins as we're finishing up dinner. "Did I understand you correctly—that you and Blake aren't seriously dating?"

"Not seriously. Although I haven't really gone out with anyone else for a long time, I've made it clear to Blake that we're only just friends."

"Just friends?"

"Well, Blake wants that to change. At least it seemed that way. To be honest, I'm not even sure."

"So he won't mind that we went out tonight?"

I shrug. "I don't see why. I told him about the premiere."

Lionel seems relieved. And, once again, I feel slightly off balance. I'm wondering what our conversation implies. Does going out with Lionel tonight send the signal that I'm interested in dating him? *Am* I interested in dating him? Is this *really* a date? Well, of course it is. When a girl dresses up, gets the car door opened for her, is taken to a nice restaurant and film . . . Of course, *that's a date*. Who am I fooling?

As we go out to the car, I wonder what this means in regard to Blake. I remember how he kissed me after our Valentine's date last month—our first kiss after the breakup last year. He's given me a few good-night kisses since then too. Nothing too heavy, since he knows I'm still being cautious. Plus, we've never said anything about being serious. Or about being "exclusive." I'm not ready for that anyway. Does Blake even care that I'm with Lionel tonight? And if Blake doesn't care ... *do I?*

I push these conflicting and confusing thoughts out of my mind as Lionel drives us to the theater. I know I'm being obsessive. And, I remind myself, I will be in Paris in a few days and I won't need to think about either of these guys. Just enjoy the moment. *Menez la vie.*

Andy's film turns out to be even better than I remembered when we were still editing it. And to my surprise, we're invited to an after party in the producer's nearby apartment. By the time we find the place, a couple dozen other film students and newbies in the industry are already there. Some faces are familiar and some are not. One girl that I never really hit it off with comes straight toward us.

"Lionel!" She takes his hand. "So good to see you here tonight. Wasn't Andy's film nearly perfection?"

He nods then turns to me. "Nevada, do you remember Erin?"

Now she peers curiously at me. "Weren't you at UCLA last year? Film school?"

Without going into detail, I explain about quitting after fall term.

"Erin got the opportunity to work on a TV series," Lionel tells her.

Nevada frowns like she's bitten into something disgusting. "Oh, I remember, you're the girl who dropped out of the program to do a *reality* TV show, right?"

"Erin works on the film crew as well as on the show," Lionel continues. "It's a great hands-on experience."

"If you like that sort of thing." I swear Nevada has tilted her nose up ever so slightly.

"They're filming in Paris next week," Lionel says.

"Did I hear that you're going to be on Andy's next film?" she eagerly asks him, totally ignoring his bit of Parisian bait. Suddenly they are discussing the upcoming project, and several other people who are also planning to work on the Idaho documentary are joining in. I step away and, feeling very much like an outsider, mosey over to the refreshment table.

"Erin Forrester?"

I turn to see Andy Dresden emerging from another room and coming straight toward me. I can hardly believe he remembered my name. "Yes." I smile and shake his hand. "Congratulations on a really great film," I say quickly. "I loved it! The storyline, the cinematography, the music—everything came together so flawlessly. Really impressive!"

"Thanks. I've seen some of your work too."

"You're kidding." I blink in surprise.

"My kid sister is a big fan of *On the Runway*. She forced me to watch it once, and when I told her I knew you she went absolutely nuts. She's in love with you and your sister."

I can't help laughing as Lionel joins us. "I'll bet she's more in love with Paige than me."

"Don't be so sure." Andy grins. "Anyway, congrats to you for a hit show."

"Lionel was just telling me that he gets to be on your crew this summer." I sadly shake my head. "I have to admit to being seriously envious."

Lionel laughs. "Don't tell me you'd rather be out in the

desert eating dust and swatting flies than trekking around those fashion hot spots like Milan and Paris."

"Trust me," I soberly tell him, "I would rather work in serious film than participate in a reality show about fashion. I'm learning a lot on the set and sometimes it's kind of fun. But the truth is I started doing the TV show in support of my sister. I keep telling myself that the work experience will look good on my résumé." I make an uncertain face. "It will, won't it?"

"It would to me."

Suddenly the others are swarming about Andy and the conversation zooms back onto tonight's film and his upcoming project. And, once again, I feel like I'm on the outside looking in. But, hey, at least Andy Dresden knew my name. That was something. Still, there's a part of me that's longing to be part of this group. Oh, I love my sister and will stick with her and her show for as long as she needs me. But realistically, how much longer will that be?

Lionel walks me to the door after our date. I'm relieved that instead of a good-night kiss, he merely takes my hand and tells me to have a good time in Paris. "Maybe we can get together again when you get back," he says hopefully.

"Sure," I say with a smile. But the truth is I'm not so sure. Really, what does this mean? Am I agreeing to more than I want, or am I just making this into more than what it really is? Seriously, maybe I need to take a correspondence course — Dating 101.

Chapter 3

"We've already shipped most of your wardrobe," Fran's assistant Leah informs us as we go over the final details before our Paris trip. "It should be at the hotel before you arrive, but you know how that can go."

"And to be safe, we'll all take some extra things in our checked bags." Fran directs this to Paige.

"What if our checked bags get lost again?" Paige asks.

"That won't happen," Fran assures us. "But just in case, make sure you have what you need in your carry-on. Because the day after we arrive, we'll have to hit the road running."

"That's right," Leah confirms as she hands us hardcopies of our itinerary. "We've got you scheduled to do *Vogue Paris* on Monday morning, and that was almost pure luck."

"So we need to have it together," Fran points out.

"You're saying you want me to have everything I need to do *Vogue Paris* in my carry-on?" Paige looks skeptical.

"I'm saying just try."

"You can put some things in my carry-on," I offer.

Paige laughs. "Yeah, right. And you can show up looking like the street lady who slept in her clothes."

"We'll manage," I assure her.

"Before you go, I want to teach you both how to roll your clothes," Fran says.

"*Roll* our clothes?" Paige frowns.

"To fit more into your carry-on bags," Fran explains. "It's a packing technique."

Fran takes us to the wardrobe room where she takes a bunch of clothes off the rack. "Do you think these garments will fit in this carry-on?" She holds up a small rolling bag that will fit in the overhead storage bin of a plane.

"No way," Paige tells her. "Not unless you're a magician."

Fran takes each item off its hanger and, one by one, lays them out one on top of the next on a table. She smoothes this stack flat and proceeds to roll it into what looks like a humongous cigar, which she then manages to fit into the carry-on, zipping it closed. "Presto." She proudly holds up the bag. "I *am* a magician."

"Wow." Paige nods. "Impressive."

"So, just in case the lost baggage nightmare in New York repeats itself, roll your clothes, girls."

"Will do," I agree.

"And make sure you don't forget your passports," she reminds us.

Leah goes over some final details and then Paige and I are finally leaving the studio. "Less than two days until Paris," Paige says as we head for the car. "I can't wait."

"Are you going to do anything this weekend?" I ask.

"Benjamin wants to see me before I leave," she says as she unlocks her car. "But I think I'm going to pass. How about you?"

I consider this. "I'm not sure. I thought Blake would've called ..." I open my phone to check for missed calls, and see that I have one from Mollie and one from Lionel. Nothing from Blake.

"I'll bet Blake's nose is out of joint, Erin."

"Oh, I don't think so."

"Get real. I've seen the boy look at you. He's totally into you."

"Really?"

"Totally. Can't you tell?"

I just shrug.

"Maybe you should call him."

"Maybe ..." But even as I say this, I know I won't. Even if Paige is right, even if Blake really is into me, I'm not sure I want that. The truth is I'm not even sure what I want. I do know that I don't want to look like I'm chasing after Blake. Yet I don't want to feel like going out with Lionel has chased Blake away either. Not that I expect Blake to give up on me that easily—at least I hope he wouldn't. And that makes me wonder ... If I had to choose between Lionel and Blake, who would it be? Then I realize how ridiculous it is to even go there. Good grief, I'm not choosing *anyone*. Still, as I mentally compare the two guys, I realize they are almost as different as night and day. Blake is pretty much an open book. He's upbeat and funny and a good encourager. Whereas Lionel is harder to read. He tends to be a realist, slightly pessimistic, and artsy. And he wants to be perceived as artsy. To be honest, Lionel and I are probably more alike. But is that a good thing?

When I get home, I return Mollie's call. I'm tempted to launch into my life, debating over which guy is more right for me. But

I know Mollie is on pins and needles right now because she's getting ready to tell her parents that she's pregnant. "How's it going?" I ask cautiously.

"I told Mom today," she says in a quiet tone.

"And?"

"And she cried."

"And?"

"And then we talked and she hugged me, and I think she's okay. I mean, sure, she's disappointed and in shock and stuff. But she's also excited about having a grandchild."

"That's cool."

"But now I have to tell my dad."

"Yeah, that won't be easy." I really like Mollie's dad, and I know he's going to take this hard. So far Mollie has been his perfect little princess, like she can do no wrong. But no matter how good a person tries to be, no one is perfect.

"I begged Mom to tell him for me, but she refused."

"It's probably better if you tell him, Moll."

"I know, but I also know it's going to crush him."

"Maybe it'll seem like that, at first. In time he'll get over it and he'll be as happy as your mom to get a grandchild. You know how much he loves little kids." Okay, even as I say this, I'm not sure. Mollie keeps acting like she plans to keep the baby, but I can't help wondering if that's a good idea. I wonder what I'd do if I were her. I hope I never find out.

"Do you think I should have Tony there with me when I tell him?" she asks with uncertainty.

"I don't know, Mollie." I try to imagine Mollie's dad with Tony standing in front of him with his head hanging down and hands in his pockets. Not that Mr. Tyson would do anything violent or crazy, but I know he has a temper and this could make him pretty mad. "Maybe not," I tell her. "Maybe you should wait on that."

"Yeah ... I guess so."

"So how is Tony anyway?" What I'm really asking is: How has Tony been dealing with this lately? So far he's vacillated between flaky and absent.

"He's trying to be supportive of me."

"That's good."

"And we've even talked about getting married."

"Uh-huh?" I try not to sound too surprised at this.

"I'm not going to twist his arm. I told Tony he either marries me because he loves me and wants to be a dad or he has to just take a hike. I don't want to have a shotgun wedding."

I kind of laugh. "Your dad doesn't even own a firearm."

"Funny. You know what I mean."

"Would you want to be a single mom?"

"I might not have a choice."

I almost mention the adoption option again, but stop myself. The last time I said something like that, Mollie fell apart. I know she wants to keep the baby and I'm trying to respect that, but I can't even imagine how hard it would be.

"So are you and Paige getting all ready for your big Paris trip?" I think I can hear envy in her voice.

"Yeah. We just met with Fran. She taught us how to roll clothes."

"What?"

As a distraction device, I explain the jellyroll packing technique, and I'm just finishing up when she tells me that she's getting another call. "Probably Tony," she says. "I guess I should take it."

"See you at fellowship tomorrow?" I ask hopefully.

"I'll ask Tony."

We hang up and I consider calling Blake and asking him about going to fellowship group tomorrow night. Really, I'd rather he was the one calling me. I know that's probably not fair, but it's just how I feel. I can't even explain why, because I've called him lots of times. There was just something about the tone of his voice when I told him about going to the premiere with Lionel that made me uncertain. Now I'm worried that our relationship already went to the next level without me fully realizing it. Or maybe I'm simply in denial.

Suddenly it's Saturday afternoon and Blake hasn't called once. Paige and I are all packed and ready for Paris. I let her use about half of my carry-on space, and rolling our clothes allowed us to pack more.

"Mom's on the phone." Paige calls into my room. "She's getting off work early and wants to know if we'll be around to go to dinner with her."

I consider this. "Sure," I agree. "I can skip fellowship group tonight."

"Okay, I'll tell her to make reservations."

I decide this might be the best thing for me to do anyway. After all, it is our last night to be home for awhile. Why not spend it with Mom? Besides, it allows me to avoid seeing both Lionel and Blake at fellowship group tonight. I may be making this into more than it is, but just in case, I'd rather lay low.

And it's fun to go to dinner with just Mom and Paige. I realize it's been awhile since the three of us have done something like this. We talk about the upcoming trip and Paige gives us an update on Benjamin's ongoing legal issues, but it sounds as if things are looking up for him. And, while I don't want to see him abusing his celeb get-out-of-trouble-free card,

I can tell that Paige feels relieved for his sake. Then I ask Mom about Jon. Suddenly both Paige and I are all ears.

"Jon and I are talking about wedding dates," Mom says after the waiter sets down a decadent chocolate dessert, which we plan to share. Paige and I exchange glances and I can tell she's as surprised as I am. Of course I know they'll eventually tie the knot. I guess I assumed it would be a ways down the road.

"So when do you want to get married?" I venture.

"Well, I was hoping you girls would help us pick the date." Mom toys nervously with her coffee cup. "That is, if you can squeeze us into your busy shooting schedule."

"How soon were you thinking?" Paige asks.

"Well, we're not getting any younger." Mom smiles. "We thought we'd just have a simple ceremony, maybe as early as June."

"June?" Paige's eyebrows arch. "That's right around the corner."

"Do you think it's too soon?"

Paige looks at me.

"I think we're just a little surprised," I confess to Mom. "But it's your wedding. It's up to you and Jon."

"I want you girls to be comfortable with this." Mom sets her napkin on the table. "If you think we're moving too fast, I want you to speak—"

"Erin's right," Paige says quickly. "It's up to you and Jon."

"Maybe it is too soon ..." Mom looks uneasy. "I suppose there's really no need to rush things."

"Is there a reason you wanted to be married in June?" I ask.

Mom sighs. "Well, you know how Dad and I got married in Vegas, and that was on New Year's Eve." She chuckles. "Back in the eighties it seemed like a glamorous thing to do—kind of fun and crazy. But as a little girl I'd always imagined a June wedding. Corny, isn't it?"

Paige pats Mom's hand. "Not corny—*sweet*."

"And waiting until June of next year ... well, that seems a long ways off. It's not like we want a big fancy wedding that will require lots of planning. Just close friends and family."

"You should go for it," I tell her. "Plan it for June."

"We'll check with Fran on our schedule," Paige promises. "We can go over it on our way to the airport tomorrow."

"So you really don't think it's too soon?" Mom asks again. We both assure her that we're fine with this. I know it's going to take me awhile to totally absorb this bit of news, but it's Mom's life, not mine.

"Where will you and Jon live after you get married?" I ask.

"We've been discussing that. There are a couple of options." She makes a slightly forced smile. "I don't think our condo is one of them. Although it's fine for the three of us, it would seem a little tight with a man around. Don't you think?"

Paige and I both nod.

"Then there's Jon's house. It's nice and roomy and you girls would be welcome to join us. Or, if you prefer, you could keep the condo and stay there as long as you like."

"By ourselves?" I ask. And, okay, I know Paige and I aren't exactly kids anymore, but the idea of living in the condo without Mom feels a little weird.

"We'd be okay," Paige assures me.

"Another thought is for both Jon and me to sell our current homes and get something together. Something bigger— and again, you'd be more than welcome to live with us."

"Would you really want to take that all on in your first year of marriage?" Paige asks. "I mean, selling both your places and combining households. It seems kind of risky to me."

"Risky?" Mom's brows lift.

"You know . . . in case things didn't work out."

"The marriage, you mean?" Mom frowns. "I guess I hadn't really considered that." I can tell by the way Mom's lips are pressed tightly together that her feelings are hurt, and I'm trying to think of something to say to smooth this over.

"I'm not saying your marriage won't last," Paige says quickly. "But, you know, just in case."

I feel really sorry for Mom. It's like we've both kind of rained on her parade. "I think Mom and Jon are going to have to figure out where they'll live for themselves," I tell Paige. "I'm sure they'll come up with a great plan."

"But I can't leave you girls out of the equation," Mom says quickly.

"Then I like the idea of hanging on to the condo for now," Paige tells her.

Mom looks at me. "How about you?"

I nod. "Sure. That probably makes sense—for now anyway."

Mom looks relieved. "Well, okay. That's what I'll tell Jon then."

"And go ahead and start planning your wedding," Paige says cheerfully.

"We'll get back to you on dates as soon as we talk to Fran," I remind her.

"Hey, I'm getting a great idea." Paige turns to me. "What if we do a special wedding feature on our show? We could cover designers like Vera Wang and Oscar de la Renta and—"

"Maybe you girls will want to shop for some designer

bridesmaid dresses in Paris," Mom suggests. "Because, of course, we want you both in our wedding."

"What kind of colors do you want for us?" Paige asks, eager.

"Something that will look good on you both, and that will look nice in a garden wedding," Mom tells her. "I'll trust you with picking out something appropriate, Paige. You have such an innate sense when it comes to fashion."

"This is going to be fun." Paige's eyes light up with enthusiasm. "I can already imagine the show." Suddenly Paige and Mom are discussing the best wedding gown designers and what styles would look the most flattering on Mom. As I listen to them chattering away, trying to nod and appear interested and enthusiastic, I realize that life as we've known it is about to change for good . . . and like many things lately, I'm not sure what I think about that.

Chapter
4

On our way home from the restaurant, I catch a snippet of a voicemail message that Paige is listening to. It's from Fran and it sounds like she's excited and like she's planning something special for our arrival in Paris.

"What's that about?" I ask as Paige closes her phone.

Paige flashes a mischievous smile. "Oh, nothing."

"It sounded like something to me," I tell her. "What's Fran planning?"

"It's a surprise," she tells me.

I frown. "I don't really like surprises," I remind her.

"Is it something to do with your show?" Mom inquires.

Paige nods with sealed lips.

"Come on," I urge her. "If it's about the show, I have a right to know."

"It's a *surprise*, Erin."

"I hate surprises," I tell her. "You know that. Remember the time Dad tried to surprise us with the trip to Hawaii?"

Paige groans. "Who would expect anyone to throw a fit over going to Hawaii?"

"I wouldn't have, except that I missed out on the school play. At the time I thought I was a pretty good actress and I wanted to play Juliet." I kind of laugh. "Okay, I realize now that it was probably a blessing in disguise and I'm sure the drama teacher and my understudy were relieved. But at the time, I was crushed."

"Yes, and you generously shared your heartbreak with all of us in Maui."

"Just for a day or two," I remind her.

"Erin has a point," Mom says. "If it has to do with the show, she has a right to know what's up, Paige."

"Yeah," I agree. "I mean, it's not like it's my birthday or something."

"Okay, fine. No surprises." Paige makes a face at me. "Our first show is going to be about us arriving in Paris, and the first thing we'll do when we get there is go to Salon Dominique."

"What's that?"

"Just one of the hottest beauty salons in Paris. The world for that matter."

"Why did you want to keep that from me?" I ask.

"Because Fran has made appointments for both of us."

"For . . . ?"

"For new hairstyles. Something *très français*."

"Meaning?"

"Meaning I've agreed to get my hair cut," she says nervously. "Something similar to Grace Kelly."

"Really?" Mom glances at Paige in surprise.

"I know." Paige nods. "A bold step."

"That's the surprise?" I ask.

"I told Fran that you'll get your hair cut like Audrey Hepburn when she played Sabrina."

"You told her *what?*" I touch my shoulder-length hair, which had been long until last December, when Paige decided it needed to be chopped. And, okay, maybe she was right. But to cut more . . . I'm not so sure.

"I thought we agreed on this, Erin."

"What?"

"That if I cut my hair, you'd cut yours. Remember when we were watching *To Catch a Thief?*"

"Yeah, but I thought we were kidding."

"I think it sounds like fun," Mom says as she turns onto our street.

"It will be," Paige assures me. "I'm taking a bigger risk than you, Erin. I'll have more hair cut off and I'm the star of the show."

"But it's your choice," I point out.

"I can't do it if you don't." She makes a pouty face.

"Why not?"

"Because that's how we planned it. Both of us getting a new Parisian-inspired look. You have to do it."

"I think you'd look lovely in short hair," Mom tells me. "You have the perfect face for it, Erin."

"And it really will make for a great show. They're going to give us complete makeovers. Come on, Erin, it'll be fun."

"Okay, okay, I'll do it." I decide to give in. It's not like Paige is going to back down.

"You won't be sorry," Paige promises as Mom parks her car. "We'll go to Paris looking like a couple of regular California girls and we'll come home looking like—"

"Like Grace Kelly and Audrey Hepburn," Mom finishes.

"Or like a couple of French girls." Paige launches into fluent French. I know she's been listening to French CDs and practicing. That, combined with the three years she took in high school, reminds me that I'll be lost when it comes to communicating over there.

"More likely we'll look like Grace Kelly and her weird-looking kid brother," I say as we're getting out of the car. "With my hair cut as short as Paige wants, I'll probably look like a boy."

"A very chic Parisian boy." Paige fluffs the back of my hair with her hand and laughs. "Just trust me, sis. I won't let you look bad."

I try not to think too hard about that as I go to my room and check my phone messages. There are a couple of texts from Lionel. One is asking me why I'm not at fellowship group tonight. The second is telling me to have fun in Paris and to call him if I get the chance. I text him back, keeping it brief, and promise to call him when I return to LA. The next one's from Mollie, also asking about why I'm not at fellowship group. I text her back, explaining about dinner with Mom, promising to call her later.

There is nothing from Blake, and suddenly I'm concerned. He could simply be acting childish, or maybe I really hurt his feelings by going out with Lionel. Since I've considered Blake to be my good friend these past several months, even my best friend during the time when Mollie wasn't speaking to me, I decide it's time for me to call him.

He sounds a little off when he answers and so I decide to cut right to the chase. "Are you mad at me?" I ask.

"Mad?"

"You know, for going out with Lionel. Are you upset or something? Because it feels like you've been avoiding me and—"

"You mean because I wasn't at fellowship group tonight?"

"You weren't?"

"You didn't even notice I was missing?" Now he sounds sad.

"No, that's not it. I wasn't there either."

"Oh."

"So, anyway, are you mad at me about Lionel?"

"Should I be?"

"Well, no, of course not."

"Then I'm not."

"It feels like you've been ignoring me."

"I've been kind of sick. I think I've got the flu."

"Oh." Is this for real or is he trying to make some excuse? "The flu?"

"Yeah. Kind of a stomach thing. Not much fun. Mom keeps telling me I should go see a doctor. But it's Saturday, so I'll probably just wait and see how it goes."

I realize that he actually does sound different, like he's really not feeling too well. "It's not about me then? You're just sick?"

He makes a weak laugh. "Yeah, Erin, it's not always about you."

"Sorry. I didn't mean to sound like that, but I've been worried about you. Now it seems like there was a reason to be. Want me to make you some chicken soup or something?"

Another weak-sounding laugh. "Thanks, but no thanks. My stomach's not up to it. No offense, I'm sure you make a mean chicken soup. But I can barely keep Sprite down."

"Wow, Blake, I'm sorry. Do you think it's anything serious?"

He sighs. "Mom's all worried that it could be food poisoning or stomach cancer or something equally serious. You know she's kind of a hypochondriac. It's probably just the flu.

Hopefully not one of those bad strains though. I think I'd prefer food poisoning. At least it gets over with sooner."

"Now I feel really bad," I admit. "I wish I'd called you yesterday. I would've come to visit. I hope you get better soon."

"Me too."

"We leave for Paris in the morning."

"I know."

"I'll call you in the morning to see how you're doing."

"Thanks."

"You sound tired," I tell him. "I should probably let you go."

"Yeah, I'm pretty wiped out."

"Okay. You take care."

We say good-bye and hang up and I feel like such a heel. Here I've been thinking that Blake's being a big baby and acting jealous and all sorts of silly things and the poor guy is just plain sick. For sure I'll check on him tomorrow to make sure he's getting better. Maybe I can send him a get well something from the airport.

Next I call Mollie and I can tell by her voice that something is wrong. "What's up?" I ask, concerned. "You sound a little bummed."

"Yeah, that's probably because Tony and I broke up," she says glumly.

"Oh, Mollie . . ." I sit on my bed, preparing myself for what I'm guessing will be a long chat. "I'm sorry."

"Yeah, me too."

"So how are you doing?"

"I've had better days."

"Yeah . . . so tell me what happened. How did he do it?"

"Actually we both did it. It was a mutual breakup."

"Oh?"

"We got into this big fight on our way home from fellowship group tonight." She gives a halfhearted laugh. "I was actually feeling kind of hopeful and happy after hearing the message—it was about how God can turn what seems to be bad into something good, and I was thinking that was kind of like an unplanned pregnancy. I mentioned something about how this baby was going to be a real blessing and Tony started acting weird."

"Weird? How do you mean?"

"For starters, it's like he's in some big kind of denial. Like he wants to act like there is no baby, like I'm not pregnant, like life is going to be just the same as before."

"Oh."

"And when I made it clear that life as we knew it is over and done with, and that he either better get used to this new reality or just beat it, he pretty much lost it."

"Uh-huh?"

"Then he told me in no uncertain terms that he wasn't ready to be a dad and that he wouldn't be ready for about ten years, and that I should give the baby up for adoption. Naturally, I told him there was no way I was going to do that. That's when he got really mad and told me he should have a say in this—that it was his baby too and that he should have a choice about the baby's future."

"Wow." I actually don't know how to respond to this. I think Tony is partially right. And yet it's so complicated. So messy.

"What do you think, Erin? Should Tony have a say?"

"Well, it *is* his baby too. But on the other hand, you're the one who gets stuck with it so—"

"*Stuck* with it?" Her tone is angry.

"I didn't mean stuck with it *like that*."

"Look, I'm perfectly aware that *no one* seems to get this, but I am happy about this baby, Erin. I want it and I love it already. I know it won't be easy, but I plan to keep the baby and I plan to be a good mom and—"

"I know, I know," I say quickly. "You will be a good mom, Moll. What I meant was Tony doesn't really have to deal with it like you do. He's not carrying the baby inside of him. He's not the one who will have to go through delivering the baby or any of the other stuff. Maybe for that reason he shouldn't have as *much* of a say in it as you do." I pause to catch my breath, hoping that this will appease my slightly moody friend.

"Oh ... okay."

"Did you tell your dad yet?" This is my attempt to shift the subject away from Tony.

"No, he left on a business trip yesterday. I'll tell him when he gets back."

"Right. I'll be praying for you, Mollie, that it goes okay when you break the news to him."

"Thanks." She sniffs like maybe she's crying.

"Are you okay?"

"I'm just so bummed about Tony."

"I'm sorry, Mollie. Maybe it's for the best that you know where he stands."

"But I didn't expect him to act like this. I had hoped he'd want to do the right thing."

The right thing? I'm trying to wrap my head around this. What is the right thing? I guess only Mollie knows. And God. "I promise you, Mollie," I tell her. "I will be praying for you every day. That everything with you and the baby will go exactly the way God wants it to go. Okay?"

"Thanks." Another sniff. "You're a good friend."

"I just wish I wasn't going to be gone so much. I'd like to be here for you more."

"Yeah, I wish that too."

"On the bright side, it's cool that your mom knows." I try to inject some brightness into my voice. "I'm sure that must make it easier."

"Yeah. We're going to the OB doctor together next week. I'd been hoping that Tony would go with me. But I guess having Mom along will be better than going alone."

"When will you find out if it's a boy or a girl?"

"I don't know. I'm not even sure I want to know."

"Because I was thinking maybe I could find some interesting baby stuff in France."

"Oh, yeah, that would be great, Erin. I'd love my baby to have something from Paris."

"I'll just look for something that works for boys or girls."

"Cool."

We talk awhile longer and I think maybe I've cheered her up some. But as we say good-bye, I feel bad once again for not being more here for her. I know life's not easy for Mollie right now. But, really, what can I do?

Chapter
5

The town car picks us up at nine on Sunday morning. Our flight doesn't leave until 12:10, but Fran said that we need to be to LAX earlier since it's an international flight.

"What time will it be when we arrive in Paris?" I ask.

"I think the flight's about twelve hours," she tells me. "That means it'll be well after midnight Pacific time before we make it through customs and collect our bags, and since Paris is nine hours ahead, it'll actually be about nine or ten in the morning there."

"Oh." I nod as I try to absorb this. "So it's kind of like we'll miss one night."

"I plan to sleep on the flight," she says. "Hopefully I'll arrive in Paris energized and refreshed and adjusted to their time zone. I suggest you girls do the same."

Fortunately we make it through security without any of the accidental carry-on item problems we experienced on our way to New York last month. We make our way to our gate and get settled to wait another hour until boarding time.

We take turns watching our bags, using the restroom, getting snacks, and using our phones. The first person I call is Blake. I'm curious as to how he's doing. To my surprise his mom answers his cell phone.

"Mrs. Josephson?"

"Yes?"

"Oh, I thought I called Blake's cell phone. This is Erin."

"It *is* Blake's cell phone, Erin. Blake is in surgery."

"*Surgery?*"

"Emergency surgery."

"*What happened?*"

"He was suffering from acute appendicitis," she tells me in a dramatic voice. "I told him I thought something was seriously wrong, but he kept telling me it was just a bug. Then this morning, he woke up in so much pain that I called for an ambulance."

"Is he okay?"

"I don't know. It's possible that his appendix could have ruptured."

"Oh no!"

"He's been in there for a couple of hours now. I'm so worried, Erin."

"Poor Blake. He sounded pretty bad last night, but I had no idea it was so serious."

"I wish he'd listened to me. I wanted him to see a doctor yesterday. A ruptured appendix is very dangerous."

"Well, I'll really be praying for him, Mrs. Josephson. I'm at the airport right now. Our flight to Paris is supposed to board in about forty minutes. If you don't mind, I'll call back before we leave to check on him again."

"Yes, that's fine. Hopefully we'll know his condition by then. We didn't think he'd be in surgery this long."

I close my phone and just shake my head. Poor Blake! I feel a lump growing in my throat. I wish I could go and be there with him. I wish I'd been nicer to him these past few days. I can't believe I never even spent any time with him before leaving for this trip. What kind of a friend am I anyway?

"What's wrong?" Paige asks as she comes back to join me at the gate. She's got an armful of magazines, a large water bottle, and some other things.

"It's Blake," I tell her. "He's in emergency surgery." I spill out the story and try not to cry. "His mom's really worried."

Paige frowns. "That's too bad. I wish there was something we could do." She pats me on the back. "Don't worry too much. Remember when my friend Kelsey had her appendix out a couple years ago? It was no big deal."

"But his mom said his appendix might be ruptured," I tell her again.

"Whose appendix is ruptured?" Fran is joining us.

"Blake's," I tell her, quickly explaining the situation.

Fran gets a somber expression. "Oh, dear."

"I was just telling Erin about my friend who had her appendix out," Paige says quickly. "She was fine within a week."

"But if his appendix is ruptured . . ." Fran shakes her head. "I don't want to alarm you, Erin. But I had an aunt who died from that."

Now the tears are coming. "Do you think he's —"

"No, no," Fran says quickly. "That was awhile back. I'm sure that medical technology is much better now."

"Here, have some water," Paige says as she hands me her water bottle. "He'll be okay, Erin."

I quickly text this news to Mollie, who is probably in church right now. I ask her to be sure and put Blake on the church's prayer chain. Then I sit and listen to Paige and Fran's reassurances, telling me that he's going to be okay. I decide to go look for something I can send to Blake—something that might help cheer him up and show that I really do care about him. I finally stop at a rather swanky-looking gift shop, where a sign is posted: We ship anywhere.

I look around until I see a very nice model sailboat. I remember how Blake loves sailing and dreams of having his own boat someday. So I splurge—and it's not cheap. Hurrying to pay with my credit card, I fill out the sheet for shipping and write a quick get-well card, signing *Love, Erin*, then hurry back to our gate just as they are starting to board.

With Paige and Fran waiting—patiently too, considering we could've boarded first since we're in first class—I call Blake's cell again and once again his mom answers. "Sorry, Erin," she says. "There's no news."

"Oh." I swallow hard. "Well, when he comes out of surgery, please, tell him I called. Tell him I'm thinking of him and praying for him. And I'll call him from Paris, okay?"

"Okay."

"It's a direct flight and I'm guessing we can't use cell phones on it."

"The last I heard you're not allowed to."

"And it's an eleven-hour flight," I say sadly.

"Well, I'll tell him you called."

"I got him a get-well gift that I'm sending to your house," I say quickly. "It should be there in a day or two."

"That was sweet of you, Erin."

"Tell Blake I wish I was there with him, Mrs. Josephson."

"He'll appreciate that. Now you go and have a good flight to Paris, Erin. We're all proud of you and your sister and your

TV show. Don't worry, dear. I'm sure Blake will be just fine."
But I can still hear traces of worry in her voice. I'm sure she's
not nearly as optimistic as she's trying to sound.

"I'm praying for him," I finally say. "Tell him that, okay?"

"I will."

We hang up and I follow Paige and Fran as they get at the
end of the line to board the plane. Once again, I'm fighting
against the tears. I feel so badly about Blake. And I feel extremely guilty too. Why was I being so stubborn? Why hadn't
I called him sooner?

Finally, I decide it's better to pray than cry. As we're waiting in the tunnel to board the plane, I begin to pray silently. I
continue to pray after I sit down by the window, leaving Paige
the aisle seat so she can chat with Fran if she wants. I'm praying that all will go well and that Blake will be fine. But there's
a strange ache in my heart as we're taking off. When I look
down to see LA getting smaller and farther away, I wonder if
this pain inside of me means that I care for Blake more than
I've been letting on. How would I feel if I lost him?

"Can you believe how nice this first-class section is?" Paige
discreetly whispers to me. And as I look around, I realize that
this is the nicest plane I've ever been in. The seats look like
they could be in someone's living room — a very nice living
room. They have ottomans and nice side tables and everything. Yet this doesn't even cheer me up.

As we're served a surprisingly elegant dinner, I remind
myself of what Jesus said about not worrying — about how
we should trust God instead. And, although I'm trying to
do this, it's hard. I know that this will be a very long trip.
At least Fran's assistant had the foresight to upgrade our cell
phone plans so that we can use them in Paris, although she

did point out that outgoing calls are more expensive than incoming calls.

I see Fran making herself comfortable and I suspect she's getting ready to take her long nap. She hands Paige a small bottle and nods toward me.

"Fran said you should take one of these pills," Paige tells me.

"Oh no," I say quickly. "I remember when you took some in New York and—"

"No, these aren't prescription sleeping pills," she says. "It's just Benadryl, an over-the-counter thing that people use for allergies."

"I don't have an allergy."

"I know. But Fran says it will make you sleepy."

I take the bottle and carefully read the back. Finally, determining that it's perfectly safe, I go ahead and take one tablet and hope it will do its trick. All I want is to go to sleep—the way I used to sometimes when my parents took us on a long drive, like to Grandma's—and then I'll wake up and suddenly we'll be there. And I can call and find out about Blake.

Somehow I do manage to sleep for awhile. Then I wake up and, although the plane is darkened and most people are trying to sleep, I feel wide awake. I wonder how Blake is doing. My watch is still on LA time and it's past nine in the evening there now. Hopefully he's feeling much better. Surely, he's out of surgery. Maybe he's sitting in bed eating ice cream. Although that's more like they'd do for someone who's had his tonsils out. Still, I try to imagine him smiling and joking. And it does not escape my attention that I'm obsessing over this guy. I can't help wondering if I would be as obsessed over Lionel if he were in the same predicament. I've always attributed my feelings for

Blake to the fact that he was my "first love." What if he's meant
to be my only love?

I don't want to go there right now. I try to convince myself
that my obsession over Blake is purely that of a caring friend
who can't be nearby to help out. I do hope that Mollie and
Tony are there with him. Although if they are, they might not
be speaking to each other. Maybe Benjamin will stop by to see
him—after all, Blake visited Benjamin in the hospital after his
car wreck. I can imagine the attention Blake would get from
the nurses, the younger ones anyway, after word got around
that he's friends with Benjamin Kross.

I can't believe how antsy I feel when the pilot finally announces
in both French and English that we're getting ready to land at
De Gaulle airport. The flight took a little longer than Fran had
predicted. It's past one in the morning in LA. And now I realize
that I won't be able to call Blake. Not at this hour.

Strangely enough, the sun is shining in Paris. By the time
we make our way out of customs and locate our bags and get
to our hired car, it's almost eleven in the morning. And I am
exhausted.

"We'll go get checked into our hotel," Fran says after we're
piled into the town car. "The crew arrived here really late last
night, but they've had a little time to rest. They'll be heading
over to Salon Dominique around two to start setting up. Your
appointment is for three thirty, so we have time to settle in and
catch a nap if anyone is tired." She yawns, then leans back and
closes her eyes.

"Are you going to call Blake?" Paige asks as the car pulls
into traffic.

"I wish I could," I tell her. "But it's almost two in the morning there now."

"Oh, yeah." She nods. "I'd rather not think about that. Otherwise I'll start feeling sleepy." Now she's looking out the window. "Wow, can you believe it, Erin, we're really in Paris."

"Not Paris proper," Fran says sleepily. "But it won't be long."

"How far to the city?" Paige asks eagerly.

"About fourteen miles."

"You seem pretty familiar with Paris," I point out.

"I lived here for a year," Fran tells me.

"Well, you guys can sleep if you want," Paige says. "I plan to see a bit of the city. And I want to get some lunch at a sidewalk café and then I'll do some shopping and—"

"Just don't forget about the hair appointment," Fran warns. "Stay close to the hotel and don't get lost. We'll meet in the lobby at three and ride over to the salon together. So don't get carried away with shopping, Paige. It's easy to lose track of the time in a place like Paris."

"How about if I hang with Paige," I offer. "I'll make sure we're in the hotel lobby by three."

"Thanks." Fran nods, then leans back, closing her eyes again.

I realize if I'm going to keep Paige on schedule I had better set my watch to Paris time. I adjust it to 11:25 and suddenly wish I had one of those watches that keeps two sets of time so I'd know when I could call Blake. Then I simply do the math and decide that I'll call him around six o'clock Paris time. That should be around nine in the morning in LA. I know waiting another six hours will not be easy.

Soon we are coming into what must be the outskirts of Paris. Buildings become taller and are closer together, traffic gets thicker, and everything looks old and interesting. Now I wish I hadn't put my camera bag in the trunk, because I'm missing some great photo ops. Fran gives Paige and me each a fat envelope.

"Euros," she explains. "I had Leah do the money changing for us. You'll need cash for taxis and food because not everyone will accept credit cards."

Fran calls out something in French to the driver and he nods. "I asked him to swing by the Gare du Nord," she tells us.

"The train station?" Paige shows off her French.

"Why?" I ask. "Are we taking a train?"

Fran laughs. "No. We're simply going by there because it's beautiful—because we're in Paris where beauty reigns. And because I have fond memories of it. You'll see."

She's right about the Gare du Nord. It is beautiful. It looks more like a palace than a train station. "Hopefully you'll get to see the inside of the terminal too," she says as the driver continues on his way. "The architecture is really lovely." Now I know I'll have to make a trip back here with my camera and hopefully get some interesting shots.

"Our hotel is in Saint-Germaine," Fran informs us.

"Is that still in Paris?" I ask with concern.

"Of course." She pulls out her map and points to a place below the River Seine. "It's this district on the Left Bank."

"And the Left Bank is *south* of the river?" I ask for clarification.

"Yes. And the north side is the Right Bank."

"So I guess it makes sense as long as you're looking toward the west." I imagine myself on a bridge over the river looking toward a sunset.

Fran nods. "That's right. Anyway, I chose Saint-Germaine

because it's near the Latin Quarter and very historical." She smiles at me. "And intellectual too. I think you're going to like it, Erin."

"What about the shopping?" Paige asks.

"Of course there's shopping," Fran assures her. "It's Paris after all. And there are some lovely cafés and bookstores, and our hotel is very close to Jardin du Luxembourg." I'm not sure if it's my imagination or if Fran is actually starting to use a French accent.

"She means Luxembourg Gardens," Paige informs me like I didn't know that *jardin* is French for garden. Okay, I realize her French is way better than mine, but I should be able to figure things out.

"You'll find lots of good photo ops around the hotel neighborhood," Fran tells me.

"But shopping?" Paige persists. "Is it really good?"

"Saint-Germaine will give you an authentic taste of Paris," Fran says as she folds her map. "We're close enough to walk to see plenty of sites and museums. And there's always the Metro, although I don't think you should attempt it today. Let's keep our exploring limited to Saint-Germaine."

"I think Saint-Germaine sounds perfect." I'm looking out the window as our car slowly weaves its way down a narrow, charming street. I feel like I'm really in Paris now. "I wish I hadn't put my camera in the trunk," I complain.

"You'll have plenty of time to catch photos before we're done," Paige assures me as she glances at her watch.

"Just don't forget about Salon Dominique," Fran reminds us as our driver pulls up to what appears to be the final stop. "Let's all keep our phones on." Fran gives some instructions to the driver about when to pick us up in the morning, then we wait for him to unload our luggage. He piles it right onto the sidewalk and Fran sends me inside the hotel to find someone to help us with our bags.

I go to the desk and suddenly realize that my French is more than a little rusty. "Excuse me," I say. "We need help with our luggage."

The woman gives me a very blank and slightly irritated look like she doesn't understand a word I'm saying. I find it hard to believe that she doesn't know at least a little English. Even so, I strain my brain to remember some French—*help with bags*, how hard can it be? "Uh ... *aide* ... um ... *avec* ... uh ... *bagages?*"

"*Font vous ont besoin de l'aide avec vos bagages?*" she says quickly—so quickly that I really don't understand much more than *avec vos bagages*, which sounds close enough to me.

"*Oui!*" I nod eagerly, "*S'il vous plait!*" At least *please* is fairly easy.

She rings a bell, calling out to someone—in French, of course.

"*Je m'excuse,*" I tell her slowly and apologetically. "*Non parlez français ... non bon.*" My French isn't very good.

"*Oui, oui,*" she says with a tiny bit of empathy. "*En fait votre parler du Français est terrible.*"

Okay, I'm pretty sure she just told me my French is terrible. Well, fine. But I'll keep trying. A man comes out from a backroom and I call out, "*Merci beaucoup,*" to the slightly snooty woman. As I lead him outside I think maybe I should stick to three phrases: 1) please, 2) thank you, and 3) I don't speak French too well. Although I suppose the old *où est les toilettes?* might come in handy too. In fact, I could use a restroom right now!

Chapter
6

Because this is a small hotel, we all have separate rooms, and I must admit that I don't mind a bit. When I share a room with Paige, her stuff usually takes over. It's rather nice having my own, albeit small, closet and bathroom. Fran pretty much just dropped her bags and took off. Paige thinks she's off to meet an old French lover. I think she simply wants to experience Paris again without dragging us along with her.

Paige's plan is for us to get cleaned up, which means she's redoing hair and makeup and changing her clothes, as well as putting some things away. At high noon, we will meet in the lobby and venture out to the streets of Paris. Naturally, I'm early. I dug out my English-to-French translation booklet and I'm walking around the lobby practicing phrases and hoping that I won't embarrass myself too much today. If all else fails I might just keep my mouth closed and attempt sign language.

"*Prêt à aller?*" Paige says when she joins me.

It's vaguely familiar, but I'm still not sure. "Huh?"

"Ready to go?" she interprets her French for me.

I nod. "*Oui.*"

"Fran said Gerard Deral isn't too far from here." Paige pauses on the sidewalk to pull out her map.

"What's that?"

"A *très chic* clothing store. Although you might even like it."

"How about if we get something to eat first?" I suggest.

I can see Paige's reluctance in the way she presses her lips together. Of course, she'd rather shop than eat, but my stomach is rumbling. "Come on," I urge her. "You'll need energy to shop."

We walk a ways and when I point out a charming café with linen-covered tables on the sidewalk, Paige can't resist. Before long we are trying to interpret the menu. And, with Paige speaking for both of us, the waiter, an attractive older guy, seems to fall under her spell. No problem if her French isn't perfect. He even attempts speaking to us in English, which I've heard is unusual in Paris. And he's so enamored with my sister that he even brings us something we didn't order.

"*Les hors-d'oeuvres complémentaires,*" he tells Paige.

"*Merci beaucoup,*" she says sweetly back. After he leaves she quietly tells me the appetizers are complimentary.

"Does he think you're a celebrity?" I quietly ask as I sample a tasty little parcel with mushroom, herbs, goat cheese, and a bit of pastry around it.

"Perhaps." She smiles.

I laugh. "Well, actually you kind of are."

The waiter is very attentive, but disappointed that he can't talk us into wine. I draw the line there for both of us. "We still have a show to do," I remind her. "You can't show up at Salon Dominique with a slur in your voice."

She gives me a disdainful look. "One glass of wine would

not make me slur." She smiles. "If anything it would only make me *très Français*."

"Even so." I firmly shake my head. We do let the waiter entice us to eat dessert and we both order espresso to go with it.

"I feel so Parisian," she says as she holds up a tiny cup of coffee.

Soon we're done and I'm trying to keep up with Paige's longer legs as she hurries toward the street where the "good" shops are supposed to be located. And while we find some bookstores, which interest me, and I even stop and get some photos of a very old church, Paige becomes more and more frustrated when we cannot locate the clothing stores.

"You're not helping," she tells me as I continue shooting interesting angles of this old cathedral.

"Hey, I'm just waiting for you to figure it out," I tell her as I snap another one. "If it takes you much longer I might just decide to go inside this church to check it out even more."

"Go ahead," she tells me in a cranky tone. "It's not like you want to shop for clothes anyway."

"That's true." I consider this as I look longingly at the church. "Do you really want to be on your own? You're not afraid you'll get lost?"

She nods firmly. "Even if I did get lost, my French is a lot better than yours and I can always ask for directions."

I check my watch. "Well, you only have about an hour now anyway."

She frowns.

"We promised Fran we'd be at the hotel by three."

"I know. And right now we're just wasting time."

"So you'll be there at three?" I persist.

She adjusts her Gucci sunglasses and nods. "Absolutely. I

have my phone. Worst case scenario I'll get lost and you guys can pick me up on the way."

That makes sense. I agree, and Paige and I part ways. My first stop is to see the interior of the church. I notice the international sign for "no photos" and so I put my camera in the bag and simply go inside the large stone building. Even though it's Sunday, it seems to be the time of day when no services are scheduled. The cavernous space is quiet and cool, and I decide to slide into a pew in the rear of the church. I don't know what denomination it is, and as I sit down I realize I don't care. To me it feels that God is here. And that's all that matters.

I bow my head and think of Blake. I've been trying to push worry about him from my mind, but now I want to take time to really pray for him. And, although I know that God listens to my prayers no matter where I am when I pray them, I feel like maybe this is even more special. I ask God to take good care of Blake, to help him to get well quickly, to not let any complications arise, and to lift his spirits. After I finish praying for Blake, I pray for Mollie, and Tony. I even pray for Mom and Jon and that God would help us all to get the wedding plans together. And then I say amen—aloud. The sound of my voice echoing in this large space actually makes me jump.

I get up and walk around, admiring the tall stained-glass windows that depict scene after scene from the Bible. They're really remarkable. And, if my French is accurate, according to a brass plaque, these windows are more than three hundred years old, although some repairs have been made in the past century. I'm amazed at how old everything is here. Compared to LA, where hardly anything is really old, Paris is ancient. It's like I can feel the history as I walk down the narrow street.

Despite the modern cars and Vespas and contemporary clothing, it's like I can imagine the people of a bygone era going about their daily business.

I'm about to cross the avenue to get a photo of a quaint-looking bookstore, when I notice a shop window filled with baby clothes and toys, and I remember my promise to Mollie. I go inside and, despite my lack of knowledge of babies as well as French, I emerge with a heavy bag and lighter purse. I know Mollie is going to love everything! I continue along, taking photo after photo and finally pause to check my watch to discover that it's a quarter till three.

I pull my map out of my bag, getting my bearings and checking street signs, to discover I've wandered a fair distance from the hotel. I figure out what looks like the quickest route back and begin to walk. I'm only halfway there when it's nearly three. I call Fran to give her a head's up.

"I'm sorry," I breathlessly tell her. "I should be there in about five more minutes if I run."

"And Paige is with you?"

"Uh ... no. She's not back yet either?"

Fran says something in French—it sounds almost like swearing. *"You lost Paige?"*

"We went our separate ways." I'm jogging now.

"But we have a show to do."

"I know." I turn a corner and narrowly miss running into an old woman with a bag of groceries. "Just call Paige, figure out where she is, and you and I will swing by and get her in the town car, *okay?*"

Another French expletive.

"I'm only a few blocks away," I huff. "In a couple of minutes, I'll be there. I'll jump in the car and we'll be on our way."

Unfortunately, it takes more than a couple of minutes. Fran does not look pleased. "This is how you want to look for the show?" she asks as I hop into the town car.

"Hey, I'm just the camera girl," I remind her.

"It'll take an extra ten minutes to get Paige," she says with irritation. "And that's if there's no traffic."

"I'm sorry," I tell her. "Paige was desperate to shop. And I wanted to visit a church."

Fran softens a bit. "I know you girls aren't interested in the same things, Erin. I chose Saint-Germaine more for you than for Paige. I hope you appreciate it."

"I do," I assure her. "But in a way it makes it harder because there's so much I want to see around here. Yet I know I need to help keep Paige on track."

"Poor Jiminy Cricket."

I just sigh and lean back, attempting to relax. I think if I closed my eyes, I might actually go to sleep. Fran is rambling on, saying how the crew is already at the salon, set up and waiting for us, and how even Luis and Shauna are there (our hairstylist and makeup artist) so that they can learn some new tricks of the trade. "Do you have any idea how much all this will cost—or what a waste it will be if we don't get a show out of it?" she demands. "What if Dominique loses his patience and decides not to go along with the show after all this trouble? Sometimes the French are like that. Impatient with Americans, refusing to put up with our bad manners. *What then?*"

"I guess we'll just come up with another show," I quietly suggest. "Or a different salon. Anyway, it doesn't really help to freak over it."

She lets out a long deep breath. "Yes, you're probably right."

Fortunately, the traffic isn't too bad and after ten minutes, we pick up Paige and I wonder how she possibly managed to collect so many shopping bags in only an hour's worth of time.

"Hey, what's in the bags?" Fran asks hopefully. "Anything we can force Erin to wear while we're recording the show at the salon?"

Paige looks at me and frowns. "Good grief, is that what you're wearing for the show?"

"I didn't have time to change," I admit. Paige still looks perfect in her powder pink linen dress topped with a dove gray jacket. Even her shoes (kind of a Pepto-Bismol pink) match her Kelly bag. Obviously the girl is dressed to impress. So what else is new?

Now Paige is digging through her bags, finally extracting a black denim jacket and a little white linen shirt, both of which are actually pretty cool. "Here, try these. They're probably more your style than mine anyway."

"Do I change right here in the car?" I ask, looking over my shoulder as if I expect some paparazzi to zip up and snap a photo of me.

"No one's looking," Paige assures me as she removes a tag.

So right there in the backseat, somewhere in Paris, I'm suddenly topless. Well, I have on my bra. Paige helps me into the clothes and does some repair work to my face and hair, and about two minutes before we arrive at Salon Dominique, I'm fairly well put together.

Fran smiles at Paige. "You know if the TV show or even acting doesn't work out for you, you could always get work behind the scenes—wardrobe, makeup, hair ..."

Paige frowns. "Are you suggesting that my job's on the line?"

Fran laughs. "No, no, not at all."

When we go inside Salon Dominique they are ready for us. And, thankfully, no one even mentions that we're a little bit late. With cameras rolling, the owner, Dominique, greets Paige as if she's a long-lost love. And she dishes it right back to him. She gushes over his salon and his reputation and basically just schmoozes with everyone in what sounds like fairly fluent French, although I can tell by their expressions that some of them are struggling with some of her words or maybe it's her tenses or pronunciation. But no one is rude.

"Now, Dominique," she says sweetly in English. "Because this is an *American* show, we need to use as much English as possible. Do you speak English?"

"But of course," he assures her in a thick accent. "Many of my clients only speak English."

"Very good." She nods.

And then he gives us a more complete tour of his salon, which is actually rather expansive and offers everything and anything a person could want. With separate areas for hairdressers, cosmetologists, masseurs, makeup artists, manicurists, and even spa facilities, I think it would take a couple of days to utilize all their services.

Finally we're back in the hair area and Paige is showing Dominique some photos she downloaded onto her phone from the Internet.

"Ah-hah," he says with raised brows. "You want to look like Grace Kelly." He looks at her and nods with approval. "Yes, I can envision that with your beautiful face." He touches her long hair. "You are willing to sacrifice, no?"

Paige nods uneasily. "Yes ... I wish there was enough to donate to Locks of Love."

"Locks of Love?" He is confused, but then says something in French to a woman who's been helping with interpretations when we get bogged down. Using her hands she explains and he seems to get it.

"Ah, yes," he tells Paige. "Well, maybe there is enough hair to help someone. We will see."

Paige points to me. "And we want Erin's hair to look something like this." She holds out her cell phone again.

He chuckles and rubs his chin. "Ah, yes ... Audrey Hepburn in the film *Sabrina. Très chic.*" He smiles at me. "Ramone will make you most beautiful, *mon cheri.*"

I thank him in French and the next thing I know I'm wearing a black haircutting cape and a short wiry man is running his fingers through my hair and nodding eagerly as he darts about his styling station. He rattles on in very fast French, which I cannot, of course, make heads or tails of. But his enthusiasm is contagious and so I just nod. Really, what choice do I have? Paige already told me that I can trust her.

Luis (our regular hairdresser) watches with a hard-to-read expression, and the cameras continue to roll as Paige and I get shampooed and before long, scissors begin to snip-snip. Fortunately, the cameras are much more interested in Paige than me and she keeps the cheerful bilingual banter going. So, pretending that none of this is really happening, I simply close my eyes and, entrusting my fate into the hands of a man who appears to speak only a few words of English, I nearly fall asleep.

"Voila!" Ramone proclaims loudly—probably to wake me—and I open my eyes to see a stranger in the mirror. My hand flies up to touch my short-short hair and I am speechless.

"You no like?" Ramone's happy smile fades.

"No, no ... uh ... *je l'aime*," I assure him in slow, laborious French. "It's just, uh ... *c'est different*." One year of French is really not much good, but all the same, I'll try. I recall how many French and English words are nearly the same except for pronunciation. So I'll imitate my sister and simply try to put on a good French accent.

"Ah ..." He nods then, and, seeming to understand my language barrier, speaks very slowly. "*Mais il est un bon différent.*" He's saying it's a *good* difference. In other words, an improvement.

"Yes ... *très bon.*" I know he did a good job, but I'm just not sure how I feel about it. I stare at my image in the mirror, trying to absorb this strange new look. For one thing my hair looks a lot darker. The bangs are very short, and he's used some kind of product to bring out my natural wave. Also, it's very short in back and I think he actually shaved my neck, which feels very weird.

I try to remember the correct words in French then quietly ask Ramone, "*Je ressemble un garcon?*" Meaning: *Do I look like a boy?*

He throws back his head and laughs loudly. "*Non, non! Vous êtes très de femme. Et très beau.*"

I'm not totally sure, but I think he just said I look *very* feminine *and* pretty. What's not to like about a compliment like that?

"Oh, Erin!" Paige has turned around to stare at me. "You look *fabuleux!*"

"Really? You like it?"

"I love it. You are totally Audrey." She frowns. "In fact, I think I'm jealous."

I really study her haircut and I'm not sure that it looks

better than her long hair. Not that I'm going there now. It's not like she can glue it back on, although I suppose she could get extensions. "You look *très chic!*" I tell her. And, of course, that's not untrue. She always looks very chic.

"Turn back around," Dominique commands. "Our work here is not finished."

Ramone then removes my haircutting cape. *"Maintenant il est fait. Fini."*

The camera crew is focusing in on me now and Paige, with her back to me, tells me to talk about my new do.

"It's very short," I tell the camera as I touch the back of my bare neck, "and it might take some getting used to. But I think I like it."

"Now you can run along and get started on your facial," Paige tells me. "I'll catch up with you in makeup."

A middle-aged woman named Adrienne escorts me to another area and soon my face is covered in some green slime that smells like mint and rosemary. It looks scary, but it actually feels pretty good. I make a face for JJ, the cameraman who followed me in here. I encourage him to go back and check on Paige. "She's the star, you know."

He winks at me but continues shooting for a couple of minutes before he eventually moves on. I lean back in the comfortable chair and, closing my eyes, I actually do doze off. I wake to Adrienne gently removing the green slime from my face. "Voila," she proclaims. "Beautiful skin, Erin. Take care of eet and eet will take care of you."

Finally I am in makeup, the last stop in this beauty relay. A pretty young woman named Odette works on me. She doesn't seem to speak much, if any, English. I'm hard pressed to make her understand that I prefer a light touch with makeup.

"*J'aime naturel*," I try. *I like it natural.*

"*Oui, oui.*" She nods and smiles as she layers on the eyeliner. "*Vous regarderez comme Sabrina.*"

I suddenly realize her goal is to make me look as much like Audrey Hepburn as possible. And I'm pretty sure Odette is going for the *after* version, not the *before*. Because I remember how the film begins with Audrey/Sabrina as a young fresh-faced girl, who then goes off to Paris, only to return home as a beautiful woman.

I'm not sure about this dramatic eyeliner and blue eye shadow. And I can tell that Shauna (our regular makeup artist) is highly amused, since she knows how I prefer a light touch. Well, at least makeup washes off. Maybe tomorrow I can look like the before *Sabrina* version again ... well, except for the hair. I'm pretty much stuck with that for awhile.

I lift my arm to check my watch as Odette does something to my eyebrows. It's a little past five now. That would be around eight in LA. Probably still a bit early to call and check on Blake. Instead, I close my eyes and silently pray for him again. *Please, God, let Blake be okay. Take good care of him. Make him completely well.* But even as I mentally say *amen* I feel a tight, worried knot in the pit of my stomach. What if he's *not* okay?

Chapter 7

While Paige and I were being pampered and prettified, Fran made a quick dash back to the hotel to pick up some outfits for us. And just as Paige is almost finished in makeup, Fran returns. She gives some quick instructions to our crew and suddenly they are gone.

"We're going to do a photo shoot of you girls." She hands me a garment bag. "Using the Eiffel Tower and Arc de Triomphe as background. The light should be pretty good for the next hour or so. You go ahead and get changed into this and I'll see if we can hurry your sister along."

"Do I get to take photos too?" I ask.

"Not this time, Erin. This is just two pretty girls in Paris. JJ will get still shots while Alistair and Gordon film the entire thing for the show. Similar to the photo shoot scenes from *Funny Face*."

"Interesting."

"It was Paige's idea, and I think it's a good one." She gives me a nudge. "Hurry so we catch the good light — or else we'll have to do the whole thing tomorrow."

Paige and I quickly change and are heading out the door when I notice a couple of familiar faces coming toward us.

"Eliza and Taylor!" Paige exclaims.

We barely exchange a greeting with our model friends from New York, and are reminded that they're here for a fashion show, before Fran herds us toward the waiting car. She shoves her business card toward Taylor. "Give us a call and we'll catch up with you girls later." She waves and hops in.

"I forgot that they were going to be in Paris," I admit. "What were the odds of running into them like that?"

"Slim," Fran tells me. "Maybe we can schedule a little get-together with them before we all meet up again at Dylan Marceau's show on Friday."

"How about four girls on the town?" Paige suggests. "We could do some serious shopping — maybe even include it in one of the episodes."

"Or if we got lucky, we might get enough material for a whole episode," Fran says as she speaks into the audio memo program on her iPhone. "A title for an extra episode: *Four Girls on the Town*. We do some power shopping at the best boutiques, maybe some friendly fashion competition followed by a lunch. Shoot lots of film." She puts her phone away and turns back to us. "Now, I want you two to pretend you're print models for this. Hopefully this will be dual purpose. We'll have a fun segment in the *First Day in Paris* episode and we'll also collect some publicity photos." She points her finger at me. "And, yes, I know you're not that comfortable with being center stage, but it's time to get over it, Erin. You need to co-operate so we can get this. Okay?"

Now I'm feeling even more nervous and pressured and I'm wondering how the tables got turned so quickly. "But I thought I was supposed to be Camera Girl," I protest. "That's what I signed on for."

Paige's brow creases. "You know, she's got a point, Fran. Why not let Erin have her camera with her and go ahead and take still shots?"

"But I wanted—"

"And the crew can get shots of her while she's taking shots of me," Paige persists.

Fran frowns. "But she looks so great. I wanted to get footage and stills of both you girls."

"Look," I say quickly, because I see the camera crew's van up ahead and I think we're almost there. "How about if we do both? For starters, I'll be camera girl and maybe that'll help me to relax a little. I'll watch what Paige is doing and suddenly I'll set my camera down and join her—like, hey, she doesn't get to have all the fun. How's that?"

Fran reaches up to give me a high five. "It sounds perfect. And you don't even need to really shoot, you can just pretend." She opens the door. "Okay, now let's do this, girls."

We're barely out of the car when Alistair is yelling at us to hurry over where they've set up on the lawn by the Eiffel Tower. "We need to move fast," he tells us. "We only have an hour or so of good photography light left. If we don't get this today, we'll have to start over tomorrow."

So Paige goes into action, strutting and posing and acting like she's the hottest thing in town. I've got my camera, but I'm shooting real shots. This is the Eiffel Tower, after all; it's not like I'm going to let this opportunity pass me by. But I also keep my word and after about half an hour of shooting, I hand my camera over to Fran and march over to where Paige is posing.

"Hey, you look just like Grace Kelly!" I strike what I hope is a stunned pose with one hand on my cheek, like, "Oh my!"

"Hey, you look just like Audrey Hepburn," she tosses back at me, striking the same pose.

Then we really ham it up for the cameras. We speak in French and act totally sophisticated, striking over-the-top poses, which probably look pretty silly. We pull out sunglasses and act like tourists and make nutty comments about the Eiffel Tower and how many pop cans it would take to build another one.

"I heard there were people who thought this tower was ugly when it first went up," Paige tells me. "Some wanted it torn down."

"Really?" I look up at the structure and shake my head. "I really like it. Maybe architecture is like fashion—one person's chic is another person's shabby." We strike some more poses and I realize this is actually kind of fun. It's like the cameras aren't even there. We act like we're competing for camera time—taking turns striking poses for Alistair, trying to see who's better, although it's fairly obvious that Paige is in charge.

I can tell we're both pretty tired and probably in need of some serious sleep, and we start getting goofy. We sing the only French song we can think of—*Alouette*—and then we begin to do a jig to it. Finally we link arms and skip around on the grass like children.

"Okay," Fran calls out. "Cut—cut. That's a wrap."

I check my watch to see that it's past seven—and that means it's around ten o'clock LA time. I head straight for my phone and while the crew is packing it up and Fran is going over tomorrow's plan with Alistair and Paige, I call Blake's number and hope his mom is still fielding his calls. To my surprise, Blake answers in a drowsy-sounding voice.

"Blake!" I cry out. "Are you okay?"

"Erin?" he says sleepily.

"Yes. I'm in Paris."

"In Paris?"

"Yes. Remember?"

"*Where* in Paris?"

I can't help smiling. It's so like Blake to ask something like this. "Right next to the Eiffel Tower."

"Is it really big?"

"Yes. But enough about me. How *are* you?"

"I'm actually feeling pretty groovy. Or maybe it's these drugs. Man, did I have some hallucinations last night. You didn't pop in to visit me here, did you?"

I laugh. "Maybe in your dreams."

"Uh-huh ... maybe so."

"But, really, *how are you doing?* It sounded pretty serious when I talked to your mom yesterday."

"Was that yesterday?"

"Yeah. You were in surgery just as we were leaving for Paris."

"Oh, right."

"But you're okay?"

"Okey dokey."

"You sound pretty sleepy," I tell him. "Maybe I should let you get some rest."

"Yeah, I'm kinda drugged up right now."

"Just call me back when you're more together, okay? Outgoing calls are pretty expensive here in France."

"You're in France?"

I have to laugh. "Yes, I'm in France. Paris, France."

"By the Eiffel Tower," he says slowly.

"Yes, Blake. By the Eiffel Tower."

"Blow me a kiss."

I giggle then blow a kiss. "There," I tell him. "Did you get that?"

"Uh-huh."

"I really should go. Call me later, okay?"

"Uh-huh ... and you know, Erin ... I love you."

"Oh ..." I consider my response. The poor guy has just been through an ordeal, he's drugged up and has probably been in a lot of pain. What can it hurt? He probably won't even remember it. "I love you too, Blake. Now get some rest. *Au revoir, cheri.*" I hang up.

Okay, I feel a bit uncomfortable telling him that I love him. It's not like it's untrue. I love him like I love my sister or Mollie. Or maybe it's even something more. But I don't need to think about that right now. I check messages and see that Mollie texted me, promising to visit Blake and to give me an update later today. Then it's time to get back into the car.

"Are you girls too sleepy to enjoy going out for dinner tonight?" Fran asks as the driver navigates through the heavy traffic.

"I'm starting to feel kind of spacey," I admit. "Like maybe I should get some rest." I tell them about my crazy conversation with Blake. "At least he's alive," I say finally. "But he sounded pretty weird ... kind of like how I'm feeling now. Kind of like I'm sleepwalking."

"Me too," Paige says. "As much as I'd love to see the night-life of the city, I think I'll have to wait until tomorrow."

Fran looks relieved. "Great. Then we'll just order room service tonight and we'll all be fresh for tomorrow's show."

"What's on the docket for tomorrow?" I ask sleepily.

"We were going to do *Vogue* first thing, but they've re-scheduled us for Friday. Now the first thing we have is Her-mès at eleven. Let's meet in the lobby at nine thirty to go over the plan."

"Hermès!" Paige sighs happily. "I want to be in top form tomorrow."

"Hoping they'll make a special Paige bag?" I tease.

"They usually use the last name," she says in all serious-ness. "So it would be the *Forrester bag*. And that way you could pretend it's for you as well, little sister."

Fran laughs. "Don't hold your breath on that one, Paige."

Just as we arrive at the hotel, Paige's phone rings and I can tell it's Mom. As Fran and I unload the car, Paige gives Mom a quick update then hands her phone over to me so I can say hello and assure her that all is well here in Paris. Then all three of us haul Paige's shopping bags and the wardrobe items that Fran brought to the salon up the elevator and to our rooms.

By the time I close and lock my door, I am so tired I can't even see clearly enough to read the menu—and, oh yeah, it's in French. I honestly don't think I can stay awake long enough to wait for room service anyway. I just take a shower, then fall into bed, exhausted.

It's dark when I wake to the sound of my cell phone ring-ing, and it takes me a few seconds to remember where I am as I roll over to grab my phone and, without bothering to check the caller ID, I answer. The clock by the bed says 5:33. "Hello?" I mumble into the phone.

"Erin?"

"Blake?"

"That didn't sound like you. Are you okay?"

"It's me." I sit up in bed. "Just sleepy."

"Did I wake you?"

"Uh . . . yeah. It's like five-something in the morning here."

"Oh, right. I forgot about that. It's about eight thirty here."

"At night?" I'm still trying to get my bearings.

"Yeah. Maybe I should call back later."

"No, no," I tell him as I get out of bed and turn on the light. "I'm awake now."

"Thanks to me." He sounds glum.

"It's okay," I assure him. "Now, tell me, how are you doing? How did the surgery go? Are you still in the hospital? Still drugged up? I want the full update."

"I'm actually feeling okay. And, no, I'm not drugged up. The surgery went really well, considering."

"Considering?"

"You know, that my appendix had ruptured. I guess that can get pretty nasty. But the doctor said the prognosis is really good. No infection. No complications. And the best news is that I get to go home tomorrow."

"Wow, that is great. I was really worried, Blake. Fran told me about someone who died from a ruptured appendix and I was starting to freak. So I just really started praying for you." I tell him about the cathedral yesterday and how it was a cool place to pray.

"Thanks. I think I could feel those prayers."

"Did Mollie come see you?" I realize that I forgot to check for messages before I crashed last night.

"She did. She told me about Tony and her breaking up. Poor Moll."

"Yeah. She was pretty bummed."

"Benjamin even came by."

"That was nice."

"Yeah ... except one of the nurses started acting all star-struck and kept making excuses to come into my room just to gape at him."

I laugh. "I suppose she's giving you special treatment now."

"I guess."

"Is she pretty?" I ask in a teasing tone.

"Not as pretty as you."

I reach up and touch my recently cropped hair. "You might be surprised if you saw me now."

"Huh?"

"I got my hair chopped off."

"Chopped off?" He sounds worried.

"Paige and I both got makeovers yesterday. Her hair is cut like Grace Kelly's, kind of like in the *To Catch a Thief* film. Mine is like Audrey Hepburn in *Sabrina*. Funny, huh?"

"I'll bet you girls look great."

I tell him about the photo shoot and how I was kind of forced into it. "But it turned out to be fun. I just hope it doesn't become a regular thing."

"I can't wait to see that episode."

We talk awhile longer and then Blake informs me that he's getting his evening check-up and meds and that he'd better go. We say good-bye and after I hang up I'm wide awake and know it'll be useless to go back to bed now. I open the drapes and look out on the predawn avenue below. All is quiet and peaceful and the street lights are still on. There's a small ter-race outside the windows with a pair of wrought iron chairs, so I wrap a blanket around me like a shawl, grab my little travel-size Bible, and go outside to sit and read ... and to con-template and pray.

The sun begins to come up and I look out over the buildings, watching as the sunlight begins to wash them with golden color. Slowly, like a waking giant, the city comes to life. People and cars begin moving down below and I can smell bread baking somewhere, and suddenly my stomach is rumbling and all I can think of is FOOD. And since this is Paris, I know that there is food—glorious food—to be found.

Chapter

8

"I hope no one is offended by my outfit," Paige says as we're riding over to Hermès Paris. It's just Paige and me in the back of the town car because Fran decided to leave early in order to have an impromptu meeting with the crew.

"You look great," I assure her. "Why would anyone be offended?"

"Because I'm wearing *Chanel*." She whispers the designer name as if this is scandalous as she smoothes the front of her tailored pink jacket. The buttons, collar, and cuffs are trimmed in chocolate brown suede and the overall look is very Grace Kelly-like. It goes well with Paige's new hairstyle.

"Really, Paige," I tell her. "You look fantastic. I even saw heads turn when you walked through the hotel lobby. And this is Paris."

"Well, I wanted to wear Hermès today, but this jacket goes so perfectly with my Kelly bag. Besides, the only Hermès pieces I own, well, besides this bag and these delicious boots"—she extends a brown leather-clad leg—"don't feel very spring-like to me."

"Well, you look fabulous," I tell her. "I'm really liking your hair. I'm sure the Hermès people will be suitably impressed." I laugh. "And if they don't like your outfit, I'm sure they'll be happy to share some of their own designs with you."

She smiles and nods. "Exactly what I'm hoping."

As it turns out, I think not only are they suitably impressed with Paige, but actually quite taken with her. In fact, our main guide, Gabin, a young designer who's also part of the Hermès family, appears to be totally smitten with my sister. Although his English is rather stilted, he does his best to keep the communication between them going as he leads us through their design studios and show rooms.

Fortunately I'm back to playing camera girl today so I'm free to simply shoot and observe—no pressure to perform. As usual, I'm slightly awed by my sister's wit and charm—not to mention her French, which seems to be improving. Even though our show is in English, she manages to keep things rolling by using her French in those moments when the language barrier threatens to slow the momentum. All in all it seems to be working.

At the end of the tour and while the film crew is packing it up and getting ready to head off to our next location, we're presented with parting gifts, including scarves and several new items of clothing, which Paige promises to wear for our show. Then to my surprise, Gabin leads me to the handbag showroom and tells me to pick out my very own Kelly bag. After carefully looking them all over, I decide on basic black. Boring perhaps, but I like it.

"*Choice excellent!*" he tells me, and I feel pleased by his praise.

"My sister is conservative about fashion," Paige explains

to him as she holds up her own Kelly bag. "She would never carry a pink bag. *Trop rose. Trop tape-à-l'oeil.*" She and Gabin laugh and I can tell that whatever she said was probably not complimentary to me. I try not to overreact. So I'm not Paige. Who cares?

"Ah, yes, but *classique* ees good for Erin." He nods to me. "She ees like French women ... a *sense of style* that ees time-less, *no?*"

Paige nods. "*Oui.* Erin resists change."

Okay, I'm not sure where she's going exactly, but I'll pretend that it's a compliment.

"Such pretty sisters you are." He folds his arms in front of him, almost as if to hint that the interview is winding down. And, really, it's time to go.

"*Merci beaucoup,* Gabin." I smile as I hold my Kelly bag and move toward the door.

"*Mon* pleasure."

Paige thanks him again and then, almost as if she wants to prolong our visit, she goes into a spiel about how our producer will send Hermès a DVD of the final show as well as information about when it will air and who to contact for purposes of advertising.

He thanks her again, saying something I don't quite understand, which Paige quietly translates for me. "He says you and I are the best form of advertisement they could hope for."

"Maybe they'd like us to advertise their Birkin bag too," I say teasingly to Paige since I have a feeling that's why she's stalling. She probably hopes that she'll score another bag. But I think it's time to go.

Out of the blue, Gabin puts his hand on my arm. "You

like zee Birkin bag, Erin?" he asks quietly with a twinkle in his eyes.

"Oh … uh, *oui*, of course." Not wanting to insult him or the handbag in question, I feign much enthusiasm. *"Oui. C'est très chic."*

"Un moment, s'il vous plait." He hurries off.

"What's going on?" I ask Paige.

She looks slightly stunned. "I'm not sure, I think he might be getting you a Birkin bag."

"Me?" I shake my head. "I don't think so."

But when Gabin returns he holds out what appears to be a Birkin bag and, like the Kelly bag I selected, it's also black. "Would you like … uh, how do you say, *faire du commerce?* You exchange the Kelly bag for these one?" He holds the larger bag toward me with an enticing grin.

I'm uncertain. "You want to *trade* bags with me?" Now I don't know a lot about these Birkin bags, but I know there's a waiting list and that they do not come cheap. I vaguely wonder if this might be a second or factory flawed, although I doubt that Hermès' high standards would allow such a thing.

"Oui!" He dangles the bag in front of me as if it's bait. "You like?"

I actually do prefer the oversized Birkin bag to the Kelly. I think it's more my style and it will obviously hold more stuff. *"Oui!"* I eagerly give him the Kelly bag and he places the precious Birkin in my hands then laughs as if this is a great little joke between the two of us. All the while I can feel Paige watching me and as I thank Gabin in French, I wonder how she will take this.

He winks at me. *"Vous êtes les intelligent."*

Now, I'm not quite sure what that meant, although I think he's saying I am smart, which is very sweet. I thank him again and Paige politely but tersely announces *it's time to go*. Holding my new bag, I follow Paige down a hall and we spot Fran in the lobby finishing up with one of the execs. She waves to us as if she'd like to say something, but, ignoring Fran, Paige walks right past her and quickly exits the building.

"What's wrong with her?" Fran asks me as we leave the building together.

I hold up the Birkin bag as an explanation.

"No way." Fran eyes the bag. "Gabin gave you girls Birkin bags? Do you know how much those bags are worth? There's a waiting list and—"

"He *didn't* give Paige one," I say quietly as I spy Paige sitting in the back of our car with her head turned away.

"*What?*" Fran looks skeptical.

"I'm the only one who scored a Birkin bag."

"Uh-oh . . ." Fran peers over at the car. "Is Paige absolutely livid?"

I take in a deep breath. "I'm not sure, but it's a distinct possibility. Do you think I should give her my bag?"

"No way." Fran shakes her head. "Gabin gave it to you, Erin. It's yours. Keep it. And be sure to use it on the show a time or two for the sake of Hermès."

"What about Paige?"

"Tell her to put on her big girl pants and get over herself." Fran walks toward the car. "If the shoe was on the other foot, you wouldn't complain."

"But I'm not Paige," I say as she reaches for the car door.

"Let it go, Erin."

We get in the car and Paige sits very quietly. Fran breaks

the silence by asking if we have a preference for lunch and Paige says she doesn't care.

"How about you, Erin?" Fran persists. "We have about an hour or so before we need to return to the hotel for a wardrobe change. What do you feel like eating?"

"It's not possible to get bad food in Paris, is it?" I ask in an overly bright tone. "Anywhere you pick is probably great."

Fran tells the driver where to take us and we just sit there silently in the backseat. Paige is looking out the window on her side. Fran sits in the middle checking phone messages. I am looking out the window on my side and wondering what to do. Part of me feels guilty and I'm seriously considering simply giving Paige the silly Birkin bag. But another part of me feels irritated. Fran is right. If the tables were turned, Paige wouldn't dream of handing over the bag to me. And that just makes this whole thing feel unfair.

Suddenly I'm reminded of other times when, as little girls, I would get something nice for my birthday or Christmas or whatever, something that Paige really liked and wanted. As a result, she sometimes made such a fuss that I would hand my prize over to her just to make peace. My payment for my generosity was that Paige would act like my "friend" for a few hours or maybe even a whole day. Then she quickly returned to being my bossy big sister again. Often I would regret giving in to her.

So as an act of stubborn defiance or French liberation, I take the petite key that's looped over a handle and unlock the tiny padlock on the front of the bag. It's so well made that it resembles fine jewelry. I remove the contents of my backpack (the very pack that Paige often complains about) and carefully load these items into the lovely Birkin bag, which is large enough to hold everything! I can't help admiring the perfect workmanship, the leather lining, the pockets, the hardware, and just everything about it. It even smells good.

"Okay, girls," Fran announces as we get out of the car. "Café de Flore is one of my favorite restaurants in Saint-Germain and I don't want you two having a catfight once we're seated. I'll go see if I can get us a table, and you settle your differences before you join me." She walks off.

"What is she talking about?" Paige asks innocently.

"I'm not sure," I say lightly. "I'm feeling perfectly fine."

Paige scowls at me. "You *should*."

"I should what?"

"Feel perfectly fine."

I pat the Birkin bag. "So you really are jealous because Gabin gave me the Birkin bag?"

"Jealous isn't the right word ..." She presses her lips together like she's thinking.

"Well, I know you wanted a Birkin bag. Maybe you should've said something."

"I should've said something?" Her eyes are angry. "What are you suggesting, Erin? That I should beg for a Birkin bag too?"

"Too?" I eye her. "Are you saying I *begged* for this bag?"

"How would you describe your behavior, Erin?"

I consider this, replaying the scene back through my mind. "I merely made a comment *to you*," I tell her. "I was speaking in English and I was joking about how we could do some advertising for the Birkin bag and—"

"That was an obvious hint and you know it."

"Fine, if it was a hint, I was hinting for your sake, Paige."

"Oh, yeah, right."

"I was. You know that I had no interest in a Birkin bag."

"You expect me to believe that? I saw you practically drooling over that bag in the car, Erin."

"Well, it is nice."

"See!" She points her finger at me.

"See what?" I demand. Seriously, when it comes to fashion and Birkin bags, I wonder if my sister needs some professional help—or maybe a fashion-freak intervention.

"I just can't believe you'd do that to me, Erin." She actually looks close to tears and, once again, I'm reminded of our childhood.

"You know, I considered giving it to you," I admit. "But Fran told me to keep it. Gabin seemed to want me to have it. And I kind of like it."

"Well, it's too big for you."

"Too big?"

"Yes. You're too short to carry a bag that size."

"Who makes these rules anyway?"

"Never mind." Paige turns and walks toward the restaurant.

I decide that's exactly what I'll do. I *will* never mind ... which means I will not worry about Paige and her crazy handbag fetish. I slip the smooth leather strap over my shoulder and, holding my head high, walk into the restaurant. And I'm not sure if it's my imagination, but it seems like people are looking at me differently, like I've suddenly turned into a real grown-up.

"Since time is a bit short, I took the liberty to order for you two," Fran tells us. "Can I assume you've sorted it all out?"

I simply nod as I unfold the napkin and place it in my lap. "I'm fine."

"Yes," Paige snaps at me. "We know that already."

I turn to Fran. "You said this was your favorite restaurant,"

I begin. "Is that because of the food? Or because it's so pretty, or what?"

She gives me a sly smile. "You really want to know?"

"Absolutely."

So Fran begins to tell us a delicious story about how she lived only a few blocks from here and how she fell in love with a French man named Renny and this was their favorite restaurant, and how she'd been perfectly happy and was willing to live in Paris forever, and then he broke up with her and broke her heart.

"Oh, that's so sad," I tell her.

"It was very sad then. I didn't think I'd ever get over it. But honestly I'm thankful now. I don't think I really wanted to live in Paris forever. And although Renny had seemed so loving and romantic and attentive, I later learned he'd been dishonest. He'd been cheating on me when I thought we were exclusive."

"The dirty rat." I shake my head.

"Yes. A rather *sweet* dirty rat."

Fran and I continue to talk about things to do and see in this district and Paige occasionally contributes something, but it's clear that her nose is seriously out of joint. And, I'm sorry, but this just bugs me!

When we get to the hotel, Fran stops me as Paige goes into her room. "Do you think she's going to be in a snit about this all day?"

"I have no idea."

"Because we still have a show to do."

"I know." I hold up my hands helplessly. "What do you want me to do? Give her the bag to pacify her?"

Fran frowns. "I'm not sure."

"Don't worry," I tell her. "Paige is good at pulling it together when the cameras are rolling. You've seen her do it enough times before."

Fran nods. "I suppose you're right."

But as I go in my room, I'm not so sure. I wonder if maybe I should simply take the high road and give Paige the bag. And, in fact, that would probably be the easiest route. I wish I could call Mom and get her opinion, but it's too early in LA. I look down at the bag, running my hand over the leather. Really, what would it hurt if I handed over the Birkin? Well, except that it might simply reinforce the idea that if Paige pouts long enough and dramatically enough, she might still get her way. Seriously, isn't it time we both grew up? I decide that, for now, I am keeping the bag.

As it turns out, I'm right. Paige does pull it together for our next visit at House of Chloé. No one would ever guess that she'd been having a pity party just a couple of hours earlier. No, Paige has magically transformed herself into sweetness and light. She even looks like a ray of sunshine in her yellow two-piece linen dress ensemble, which is, of course, a Chloé design. She seems to stand out even more than usual since all the fall fashions seem to be drab shades of brown, charcoal, and black. I get this, but it still feels a little strange when it's springtime and there are flowers outside.

As the interview winds down, I can tell by Paige's expression that she's not that impressed with the Chloé fall collection. But then these clothes aren't really Paige's style. Still, she finishes the interview with her usual flourish and the Chloé people seem totally oblivious to Paige's personal preferences, which is fortunate. We are presented with gifts, the crew wraps it up, and Fran calls it a day.

As we're heading out to our cars, I'm wishing I could go with the camera crew instead of with my sister, who seems to be turning quite frosty again. At least to me anyway. She makes small talk with Fran, but when I tell her she did a good job just now, she doesn't even say thanks. Of course, I'm aware that she's still pouting over that stupid Birkin bag. But the worse she acts, the more determined I become to dig in my heels. I imagine us in a tug-of-war with the Birkin bag serving as the rope between us. As selfish and mean-spirited as it feels, I would rather see the designer bag torn to pieces than give in to my sister right now. However, I don't really think that's what Jesus would do. Still, I'm not ready to roll over just yet.

Chapter 9

"*I have good news,*" *Fran announces as* we're riding back to the hotel.

Because Paige still seems to be quietly sulking, I ask Fran what kind of good news.

"We're all set for a shopping day with Taylor and Eliza on Thursday."

"That's nice," Paige murmurs.

"*A shopping day in Paris,*" I repeat for Paige's benefit — like maybe she wasn't listening. "You should be over the moon."

"Sure, it'll be fun."

"Paige?" I lean over and stare into her face. "You're still pouting over the Birkin bag, aren't you?"

"No, I'm not."

I roll my eyes. "You are too." I hold the bag out to her. "Here, you want it? You can have it." I dump the contents out onto my lap and shove the empty bag at her.

"I don't want your stupid bag." She pushes it back at me.

"No, I insist." I toss it back into her lap. "Take it. I don't want the silly thing if it's going to make you miserable. It's not worth it. Seriously, just take the bag and let's move on."

"I do NOT want it."

"Yes, you do," I argue. "For some reason it's important to you, Paige. You know I couldn't care less about labels and designers. *Just keep it.*"

"*I don't want it!*" She throws the purse at me.

"Girls!" Fran says sharply. "Chill out!"

Paige begins to cry. This makes me feel even worse. "Really ..." I soften my tone. "I don't want the bag. You can have it. Please."

"I don't want your bag," she sobs as she opens her own bag, retrieving a tissue.

"What then?" I demand. "Why are you being so weird about this?"

"Because I want my *own* Birkin bag."

I exchange glances with Fran and she just shakes her head like she sees our ship slowly sinking. While Paige quietly cries, I dig around the junk that's in my lap until I find a rumpled business card from Hermès. I quickly dial the number and in stilted French explain who I am and ask to speak to Gabin. To my surprise, he comes quickly to the phone.

"Bonjour, Erin. How are you?"

"*Je suis bien,*" I warmly assure him in my best first-year French. "*Et vous?*"

"I am well," he tells me. "What can I do for you?"

"I want to ask a favor," I say slowly.

"*Oui* ... I mean yes ... *anything.*" His eagerness surprises me.

"*Ma soeur* — Paige — would like a Birkin bag too. Can you please put her name on a waiting list?"

"But of course, Erin."

"*Merci beaucoup.*"

"But she must give description . . . for *couleur* and leather. Not *rose* perhaps."

I know that *rose* is pink. "Yes, I'll find out and get back to you."

"I am happy to help you, Erin."

I thank him again and say *au revoir*, then hang up. "There," I tell Paige, who is looking at me with a shocked expression. "You tell me what color and what kind of leather and whatever else there is to decide and I'll tell Gabin to order it."

"You can't afford to buy a Birkin bag," she points out.

I hold up my black bag. "If I sell this on eBay I can." I frown. "Or nearly."

She shakes her head. "No, Erin. You cannot sell your Birkin bag. I won't let you."

"It's not up to you," I firmly tell her. "Tell me what kind of bag you want or else I'll have to decide for you, and I'm sure you won't like what I pick out because *I'm so conservative.*"

"I'm sorry," Paige says softly. "I really was acting like a baby. Let's just chalk it up to jet lag and worrying about Benjamin."

"Why are you worried about Benjamin?" I ask. "I mean, aside from the usual."

"He sent me a disturbing message today."

"What's up?"

"He's freaking over the court case. His attorney wants to make a settlement with Mia's family and I guess the sum is pretty staggering. Benjamin's afraid he'll go bankrupt and lose the movie deal, and he thinks he's already lost me. He's just a very unhappy guy right now."

"At least he could be done with it, I mean, if they settle." To be honest, I'm not sure that Benjamin shouldn't be tried in a civil suit, but I am so not going there right now. And really, I don't know the details, and it's possible a settlement would be the best for all of them. "Maybe if Benjamin settles, the whole thing will die down. The bad press will go away and he might still get his movie deal."

"I guess that could happen. Really, it's his problem."

I nod. "But you still care about him, and obviously, he cares about you. I'm sure that's stressing you out."

"Yes ... still, I'm sorry I acted so childish today." She turns to Fran. "I'm sorry for being such a witch."

Fran laughs. "Well, it's a relief to know that more was going on than just a temper tantrum over a handbag. I was starting to get worried."

"I plan to take a shower and just relax when I get back to my room," Paige tells us. "I'll have room service for dinner then go to bed early. By tomorrow I'll behave much better."

"I know you will." Fran pats her hand. "We all will."

Paige turns back to me. "And please call Gabin and tell him there's been a mistake — cancel that order. *Okay?*"

As the town car pulls in front of our hotel, I promise to cancel the order.

"If I change my mind," she says as we're getting out, "I'll just order the bag myself. Who knows, in a couple of years six grand for a purse might sound like a pretty good deal."

I feel slightly faint when I hear this figure. "This purse costs *six thousand dollars?*"

"Somewhere in that neighborhood. And that's only because it's a frills bag. A nice custom bag might run around forty thousand dollars."

I stare at the bag. "That's crazy, Paige. How on earth could a handbag possibly be worth that much?"

She gives me what seems a slightly patronizing smile. "Style like that does not come cheap, Erin."

Well, I'm not sure how to respond to that. Mostly I'm still in shock. All the same, I suspect that real style cannot be purchased—not at any price. Just then I hear my phone ringing and my purse is such a mess after dumping its contents out and then back in that it takes a few seconds to find my phone. When I finally answer it's Blake's voice I hear on the other end.

"Hey, I caught you," he says cheerfully. "Am I interrupting anything? Are you in the middle of some big shoot?"

"No." I sit on the bench outside of the hotel. "We just finished up for the day."

"I just wanted to thank you for the boat."

"Boat?" I frown as I try to figure out what he means. "Are you on pain meds again?"

He laughs. "The model sailboat that you—"

"Oh, yeah," I say suddenly. "I almost forgot."

"Well, it's great. It's sitting right here on my dresser and I totally love it. Thanks."

"You're welcome. I guess I was hoping that all your pain and suffering would sail away into the sunset," I joke.

"Actually, I wish that you and I could sail away into the sunset, Erin."

I swallow hard, wondering just how much he can remember from his drugged-up conversation. "Uh … what time is it there, anyway?" I know I'm using time as a distraction, but I'm not ready to talk about sailing off with anyone just now.

"It's early. A little past eight."

"Right." I launch into the story of Paige and me and the Birkin bag. This turns out to be pretty good entertainment because I make him laugh so hard he begs me to stop before his incision breaks open.

"You're killing me," he says.

"Sorry. Actually, part of Paige's problem was that she's worried about Benjamin. Have you seen him lately?"

"No, but he left a message. Maybe I should give him a call, eh?"

"Oh, would you? That might lift Paige's spirits. She's trying to keep him at a distance, but I know she really cares about him. And then it's like he's trying to reel her back in."

"Oh, you Forrester sisters and the way you string your men along," he teases.

"Yeah, right."

We talk awhile longer and then I get another call. "Someone else is calling," I say quickly. "I'll bet it's Mom—I should take it."

"Go ahead," he says. "Thanks again for the boat."

But when I take the call it's not Mom. To my surprise, it's Gabin from Hermès. "Oh, I'm so glad you called," I tell him.

"I am glad that you are glad," he says happily.

"*Sont vous bien?*" I make a clumsy inquiry to his well-being.

"*Oui. Bien. Et vous?*"

"*Bien. C'est un jour joli.*" I know I'm stalling by saying it's a nice day in my schoolgirl French. I'm trying to think of a graceful way to tell him that I made a mistake—that I want to cancel the order for the Birkin bag. He rattles a response in fluent French and the best I can make of it is that he's talking about the weather.

"*Oui, oui,*" I tell him.

"*Parfait!*" he exclaims.

I know that means perfect, but I'm unsure as to what he's

referring to and so I decide it's time to cut to the chase. "I'm sorry," I tell him. *"Je ne parle français très bon."* I do not speak French well. "Can we speak in English?"

"Oui. I mean, yes. But my English ees not so good."

"It's better than my French," I assure him.

"So ... uh ... what time ... to come to meet you."

"To meet me?"

"Oui. For dinner."

"Oh." That's what he meant when he said perfect — I must've agreed to have dinner with him.

"Ees all right? Am I too push-ee?"

I consider this. Gabin seemed the perfect gentleman. And his connection with Hermès is important. Why shouldn't I have dinner with him? "Dinner would be nice," I tell him.

"How about, uh, *sept heures.*"

I silently count on my fingers — *un, deux, trois, quatre, cinq, six, sept.* "Seven." I say. *"Parfait."*

He asks which hotel and I tell him the name. *"Voir-vous!"* he says cheerfully.

"Yes," I say, "See you."

Of course, once I've hung up I wonder what I've gotten myself into. Just to be on the safe side, I decide to call Fran and see what she thinks. "It's a wonderful idea, Erin," she tells me. "Gabin seems like a very nice young man. Smart, creative, and well respected in the company."

"You don't think we need a chaperone or anything, do you?"

Fran laughs so loudly I have to hold my phone away from my ear.

"I'll take that as a no."

"Good. No, as long as you have your phone and taxi money — in case anything goes wrong. I don't see how there could be a problem. I'm pretty sure I can count on you not to drink too much wine."

"Too much? I won't be drinking any."

"Oh, Erin …" She makes a *tsk-tsk* sound. "Before you leave Paris, you must at least *sample* some wine."

"Don't hold your breath on that one."

"Well, have a good time. If anything goes wrong, call me and I'll rescue you." She laughs again. "Not that anything bad is likely to happen. Just go have fun and be young! After all, this is Paris—and it's springtime!"

"You're sure you don't want to come a—"

"Not on your life! But don't stay out too late. We had to squeeze an extra designer into tomorrow's schedule. It's going to be a full day."

I promise to be ready for it, then hang up my phone and head for the elevator. I'm not sure whether to consider this a date or a business dinner—most likely the latter. Whatever the case, at least I'll have time to explain about my request for a Birkin bag now. Hopefully he'll understand. I'm about to go into my room when I wonder if Paige might like to come along. I tap quietly on her door and she answers in her bathrobe. I quickly explain my unexpected dinner plans.

"You're kidding!"

"No. I was just about to call him about the bag and he called me."

"*He* called you?" She pulls me into her room. "Why did he call you?"

"Apparently to invite me to dinner."

She chuckles. "You know, I could tell he was into you. The whole time I was—"

"No way," I interrupt. "I thought he was into *you*. He seemed so interested and—"

"I caught him sneaking glances at you, Erin. You were oblivious because you were so busy filming. Now that I think about it, it all makes sense. He gave you that bag because he likes you."

I sink down to her bed. "Oh, no."

"Oh, no?"

"Well, maybe I should've said no to dinner. I mean, if he likes me and he gives me an expensive gift then takes me to dinner and—"

"I didn't mean to make it sound like that, Erin. Gabin seemed like a sweet guy. You should go out with him."

"But I don't want him to get the wrong idea." I look up at her. "Do you want to come with us?"

She laughs. "No way. I am not going to be a fifth wheel."

"Wouldn't that be a third wheel?"

"Whatever. I'm not going." She holds up her hands. "Look at me. The only place I'm going tonight is bed." She goes over to her closet, which is actually about three times bigger than mine, and begins digging. "We need to dress you up, Erin. Something fun and French."

"But I—"

"No buts."

So I give in to my personal stylist yet again, thinking at least she's not mad at me anymore. I didn't even have to give her my Birkin bag. As she helps me with wardrobe, makeup, and hair, I tell her about talking to Blake and how he's going to get together with Benjamin and how he'll try to encourage him and keep us updated.

"Dear old Blake," she says as she holds up some dangly earrings, then shakes her head.

"I just hope dear old Blake won't be upset to find out I'm dining with a Frenchman tonight."

"You don't have to tell him, Erin." She holds up some smaller pearl stud earrings and nods her approval. "Here. Wear these."

Finally, a few minutes before seven, I'm ready. "Thanks, Paige. I'm sure Gabin will appreciate it too."

She smiles. "And hopefully he won't mind that you're canceling that order. You can always tell him that I'll get back to him on it after I have time to think about it."

"What color bag would you want if you ordered one?" I venture. Okay, I know it would be crass to try to get Gabin to take my bag back in exchange for another. I mean, I've already used it.

"A soft dove gray might be nice," she says. "Or a light taupe. Something neutral but classic is always a good choice."

I nod. "I can imagine that. So you wouldn't go with pink then?"

"Hey, what can I say?" She makes a goofy smile as she picks up her pink Kelly bag. "I happen to like pink. I'm just a pink sort of girl. For me pink is a neutral. A pale pink Birkin would be heavenly."

I hold up my big black bag. "*Vive la difference!*" As I'm leaving I can't help seeing what looks like a small trace of envy — or maybe it's longing — in Paige's eyes. I go down to the lobby and think how strange it is that I'm the one dressed to the nines, carrying the prize purse, and meeting the Parisian designer for dinner tonight. I'd call Mollie and tell her all about it, only I'm sure it would make her feel envious too.

Even Blake wouldn't be too thrilled to hear about this. Finally, with a few minutes to spare, I call Mom. She's excited to hear the story, and although she gives me motherly advice about my date, she ends by telling me to "Just have fun!" And that, I decide, is exactly what I plan to do.

Chapter
10

Thanks to our language differences, my dinner date with Gabin starts out a little awkwardly. But as he drives us through the city in a very cool red Peugeot convertible, it seems like we both decide to relax and feel free to make mistakes. It's a good opportunity for him to practice his English and I practice my French—although it turns into something that sounds more like French-glish. Somehow we manage to understand each other.

After he orders our dinners, which I beg him to do for me, I tell him about film school and about how my father had been a news anchor and how my mom's a news producer. I even tell him about Blake and I actually use the B word (boyfriend), which I know is an exaggeration, but it's my way of letting Gabin know I'm not available. Not that he's asking for my hand in marriage or anything. I guess I'm just old-fashioned about things like this.

Gabin, who I learn is twenty-four (a bit older than I thought), tells me about design school, and his family (including numerous step-siblings, step-moms, and step-dads) and how they are connected with the Hermès business. Finally, as we're having a dessert of *mille-feuilles*, which are what we'd call Napoleons, he tells me about how he got his heart broken by a woman named Bernice about a year ago. He even confesses that I'm the first girl he's gone out with since Bernice. I'm not sure whether to feel honored or nervous. I hope I haven't sent any wrong signals—like accepting expensive gifts, although designers are always generous with Paige and me, since it's a form of advertising. Besides, I think I have an innate sense about Gabin. I can tell he's a sincere and decent young man.

And despite our language barrier, I have a feeling that he and I could become good friends, especially if we lived in the same part of the world. After we finish our meal, he asks what I'd like to do and I admit that I'd like to do all the silly tourist things—like driving down the Champs-Élysées, admiring the fountains and lights, or even walking along the River Seine.

"Like they do in the movies," I tell him. "Is that silly?"

He grins. "Not silly. *Ravissant!*"

So that's what we do. And he's right. The reflection of the lights on the rain-dampened avenue, and the illuminated fountains, even the cars moving slowly about the Champs-Élysées with only their parking lights on ... it's such a lovely scene—it is *ravissant*, or charming. And although I hate to end this magical evening, I know that Paige and I have a full day tomorrow. I thank Gabin and tell him that I should call it a night.

"Perhaps another time," he says as he drives me to the hotel, "we can do more tourist sightseeing."

I tell him in French I'd like that. Then, when we're just minutes from the hotel, I suddenly remember about Paige's

Birkin bag. I attempt to graciously ask if I can cancel that order. He laughs and says "no problem," and I sigh in relief.

"She did not want a Birkin bag?" he asks as he parks in front of the hotel.

I shake my head and pat my own bag. "*Non*. She wanted a Birkin bag. It's just that I didn't realize they were so expensive. I had no idea."

He smiles. "But they are nice, no?"

"*Très agréable*. And someday Paige will order one for herself."

"I wonder ... what color your *soeur* would like?"

I laugh. "*Rose*."

Now he laughs. "Ah, yes. *Rose*. But of course."

We get out of the car and once again I thank him for a lovely evening. He takes my hand in his, looking directly into my eyes. "May I call on you again, Erin?"

I feel unsure; does "call on me" signify a date? Because I did want to go sightseeing again. But a date ... well, I don't know. To confuse me even more, I think about Blake. Yet at the same time I wonder *why shouldn't I see Gabin again?* Despite using the B word, it's not like I'm in an exclusive relationship with anyone. Not Blake or Lionel. What could it hurt? Gabin is a sweet guy. And so I agree, trying to explain in my broken French-glish that I'm not looking for a serious relationship of any kind. I also remind him of my age—although I don't really feel that much younger than him. Fortunately, he seems fine with my conditions. He simply kisses my hand and says, "*Bonsoir!*"

As I go into the hotel, I understand how a young woman could get the impression that Paris is a romantic place. Not that I'm falling in love with Gabin—I certainly am not. But I could be falling in love with Paris!

The next day is scheduled tight and, as Fran likes to say, we hit the streets running. It's Christian Dior at ten. Pierre Cardin studio at one. And finally, one of Paige's favorites, Christian Louboutin at three. What makes my sister so enamored with Louboutin's red-soled, very high-heeled shoes is a mystery to me. She is totally jazzed about this particular visit. And naturally, she's dressed to the nines in a fitted cream-colored linen jacket and a beige skirt (Chanel, I think), and she's wearing her favorite Christian Louboutin pumps, which are kind of beige-ish pink.

"Clichy," the woman who's handling the interview says as she points to Paige's shoes. "Nude."

Paige nods. "Yes. I love them." They chat back and forth — part French and part English and, as usual, we make our way through the various design rooms and offices until we come to the showroom, where my sister's eyes grow wide and she is momentarily speechless. Now, while this is our usual scenario for filming these shows — finishing off with the showroom — she's acting like this is the first time she's ever seen one.

"Oh-my-gosh!" She gasps as she walks around taking in all the various high-heeled shoes. "I feel as if I've died and gone to shoe heaven. These are so beautiful! How does Christian Louboutin do it?"

I keep my camera on Paige, hoping to catch her drooling over the pair of hot pink open-toed pumps that seems to have caught her eye at the moment. But she simply sighs and slowly moves from one pair of shoes to the next, making clever commentary for the sake of the cameras. I get close-ups of the shoes. Some have animal prints, others are rhinestone encrusted, some have buckles, some have bows. There are reptile skins and shiny patent leather and velvet and just about anything a person could imagine—and more.

Finally Paige is back where she started, staring at the hot pink pumps. "I am going to have to buy those," she tells our guide. "You must have a boutique in Paris—"

"Nonsense," says a male voice, and suddenly a middle-aged guy enters the room. From the way Paige reacts, for a moment I think he's royalty. She quickly regains her demeanor. "Oh, Mr. Louboutin," she says happily. "You are so kind to join us. I didn't expect—"

"My pleasure." He steps forward, takes her hand, and smiles for the cameras. "My congratulations on your TV show. I hope to see it someday."

She thanks him in French and then tells him that he is her favorite shoe designer. She gracefully holds out her foot, pointing her toe.

"Ah, Clichy." He nods. "A good choice." He steps back and studies her as if trying to think of something. "You know, Paige, you resemble someone ... I cannot think ..."

She makes a smile that I'm sure is meant to be an imitation of Grace Kelly, and he snaps his fingers like he gets it. "A young Grace Kelly. *Magnifique!* You are just the sort of woman I design for."

She thanks him again.

"And you know," he says, "Princess Grace's daughter Caroline likes my shoes also."

"I know." Paige nods. "You have many famous admirers, including Sarah Jessica Parker, Nicole Kidman, Cameron Diaz ... just to name a few."

He waves his hand in a modest gesture. "Beautiful women ... ah, they love beautiful shoes, no?"

As Paige heartily agrees to this, I wish I could ask this
guy if he's got any concerns about beautiful women destroy-
ing their feet, injuring their backs, or even breaking an ankle
in his pretty high-heeled footware. I've worn them a time
or two and it's not something I particularly enjoy. I'm also
curious if he's ever been sued, although I doubt that's likely.

"Now is it true," Paige asks him, "that you once went to a
museum and saw a sign that said women in high-heeled shoes
were not allowed on the wood floors?"

He chuckles. "You have heard that old story?"

"I heard that you wanted to break the rules," she says in a
coquettish tone.

He laughs. "Life is no fun if you do not break some
rules, no?"

She laughs too. "I totally agree." They chat a bit more,
then he looks at his watch.

"I wish I could visit with you more," he tells her, "but
I have an appointment." He turns to our guide. "Please, see
that Paige finds the shoes she desires." He looks back at Paige
and smiles warmly. "Ah, yes, you have the beauty that inspires
good design."

As he leaves, I wonder if my sister is about to swoon.
Instead, she turns to the camera and delivers her final line.
"And Christian Louboutin has the kind of design that inspires
beauty. So, don't forget that fashion matters and always remember to put your best foot forward." She points her toe
for the last shot. "And today it's my *very best* foot—Christian
Louboutin!"

As Fran calls cut, I think that today's interview might
even make up for the disappointing Hermès visit. As the crew
wraps it up, Paige controls herself by only picking out three

pairs of shoes, because I can tell she really wants more. These are promised to be delivered to our hotel in the proper size before the weekend. No one asks me if I want to choose a pair, which is fine with me, because I'm not really that interested. Today was Paige's day. And that's a relief.

The next morning, we all sleep in. I can't speak for Fran or Paige, but I need it. The plan for the day is to meet up with the camera crew and Taylor and Eliza around noon at a Right Bank café that is well known for its fine *patisseries*—including filled croissants. After that, according to Paige, I'm about to be treated to the best shopping in Paris. I'll admit to skepticism. I'd much rather spend my time in the quaint shops near our hotel in Saint-Germaine, but I know Paige can't wait to hit the French designer boutiques. Naturally, Paige looks like she should be on the cover of *Couture* and I know she hopes the paparazzi will be around to notice. So far they haven't been a problem. And while I'm relieved, I know that Paige is not. In fact, she's worried.

Since I don't get to be Camera Girl today, Fran insisted that I dress for the part of *sister shopper*. I'm stuck in a pair of less-than-comfortable but gorgeous Prada faux-leopard-skin pumps. I am allowed to wear "nice" jeans as long as I top them with a Chanel jacket the color of butterscotch. And, of course, I'm carrying my Birkin bag, where I've discreetly tucked in a pair of flip-flops (foot relief) and my camera ... just in case. Paige and I are mic'd and prepped and ready to play our roles. Well, I'm ready to playact—Paige will simply be herself.

As our car snakes its way down a busy avenue, lined with glistening, ritzy-looking store fronts, I notice a number of well-dressed shoppers parading along. They are obviously wealthy and, like Paige, designer-driven. I can feel the resistance coming on. This is so not me. Yet at the same time I know our show is about fashion and viewers expect this. I need to get over it.

And yet I believe there's more than one kind of fashion. Already I've seen a lot of creativity, variety, and consideration for the planet (as well as the pocketbook) over in the Left Bank boutiques. I take in a deep breath and remind myself that I'm not the one calling the shots here. And, as the car stops at a corner, I prepare myself to simply bite the bullet and get on with the show. Today it will be Parisian *haute couture*.

The camera crew is already set up on the edge of the sidewalk by the café and, naturally, this is attracting a bit of attention, but not nearly as much as it would in, say, LA. Fran joins them while Paige and I, acting perfectly natural (like Fran has directed), make our way to where Taylor and Eliza (also mic'd for sound) are already seated at an outdoor table. Air kisses and greetings are exchanged, and, thanks to a ready waiter, coffee and pastries are ordered.

"You girls look gorgeous," Eliza tells us. I can tell she's got one eye on the camera and I suspect this will get cut if she doesn't act more natural. "I love your new hairstyles. Very Parisian."

Paige thanks her and talks a bit about how we had our makeovers and then a photo shoot by the Eiffel Tower.

"What fun," Taylor says. "Like a scene out of *Funny Face*."

Paige laughs. "Exactly!" She points at me. "Don't you think Erin looks like Audrey Hepburn in *Sabrina*?"

Taylor studies me then nods. "She actually does."

Then I tell them about Grace Kelly and they agree that Paige resembles her. They talk a bit about the upcoming Dylan Marceau fashion show and how, although Dylan has French ancestry, he is virtually unknown over here.

"It will be his Paris debut," Eliza says with what seems vested interest, like she is somehow personally responsible for his show. While I know her parents are influential and live in France, it's hard to imagine they were the ones who arranged all this. "He's so nervous. We're hoping that he's not disappointed."

"And you know how Parisians can be," Taylor says.

"Zay are, after all," Paige puts on a thick French accent, "zee fashion experts. It ees possible zay will look down zer noses at zer American offspring."

Taylor laughs. "*Oui*, eez possible."

"But you will be covering Dylan's show, right?" Eliza asks eagerly.

"Absolutely," Paige assures her. "I adore Dylan's designs."

"They're da bomb," I say without thinking. Then feeling silly, like I really don't fit in here, I reach in my bag for my phone, pretending to check messages, although I know there are none since it's the middle of the night in LA. After a few minutes, the waiter arrives with our coffees and pastries, carefully arranging them on the small table, almost as if he too knows he's being filmed.

Thankful for a distraction, I pick up my fork and delicately cut into my apple-and-almond–filled croissant. I decide to focus my attention on this delectable treat while the others continue to chatter away about French designers—who is hot and who is not. I nod and feign interest between bites, but fortunately, their fashion-obsessed conversation is nonstop and I doubt my absence is even noticed. This frees me up to relish every delicious crumb of this lovely Parisian patisserie.

"What happened to your croissant, Erin?" Eliza looks at me with wide blue eyes.

I shrug. "I ate it."

"The *whole* thing?" She looks slightly horrified.

"Well . . . yeah." I notice that she hasn't even touched hers, and Paige appears only to have taken a bite or two. Taylor's looks a bit more nibbled on. I feel like an ill-mannered sow.

"You're not concerned about carbs?"

"Not really." I frown at her.

"Do you realize how much butter is in a croissant?" she asks with concern. "What the fat count is?"

"Hey, lighten up," I say in a joking tone. "I mean, this *is* Paris."

"I am lightening up," she tells me. "Which is precisely why I'm avoiding French pastries."

"But the French are famous for their food and especially their pastries. Aren't you at least going to try it?"

"Are you kidding?" She looks appalled as she slides her untouched plate away.

I shake my head, controlling myself from forking into her uneaten raspberry scone. "How sad."

Taylor forks back into her croissant. "It's really delicious," she tells Eliza. "And you're absolutely right, Erin. This *is* Paris, and we should be enjoying the wonderful cuisine just as much as the fashion."

Paige doesn't look convinced as she cuts off a tiny bite. Meanwhile Eliza simply picks up her espresso, with a slightly sour expression, and takes a dainty sip. Does she think coffee has calories too?

I peer at her. "You're obviously watching your weight."

She smiles at me in a slightly superior way, a way that I find extremely aggravating. "Of course."

"Why?" I demand. "You're already too skinny."

She laughs. "Thank you."

"It wasn't a compliment," I tell her.

"Erin has a problem with stick-thin models," Paige injects. "In fact, I'm not overly fond of anorexia myself."

Eliza points at my sister's barely touched pastry. "Then why aren't you eating that?"

Paige holds her head high as she picks up her fork, cuts off a normal-sized bite, and eats it.

"I'm with you," Taylor tells me. "I think models should look more like real people. Dylan thinks so too."

"Then what's Eliza's problem?" I ask — perhaps a bit rudely. Well, wasn't she rude to tell me about the fat and calories?

"Dylan isn't the only designer," Eliza tells me. "There are some who will only hire *thin* models. I want to be ready for them."

"But they're wrong," I say. "Why would you even — "

"That's enough." Paige holds up a hand with a congenial smile that she shares with the table. "Okay, girls, enough talk about weight issues." She looks at me. "That's *another* show, Erin. Today we are simply four girls on the town. Our focus is fashion and we are going to shop until we drop. *Okay?*"

I nod my agreement. "Some of us might drop sooner than others if that's okay with you."

She laughs. "Yes, I understand completely."

"Let the games begin," Eliza says cheerfully.

And the games do begin cheerfully, with Paige, Taylor, and Eliza lightly sparring over style and design. I know enough to keep my mouth shut. Unfortunately, the sparring soon evolves into what feels more like a competitive sport, like Paige and Eliza keep trying to one-up each other. And while Paige, in my opinion, has better taste and more fashion expertise, Eliza appears to have a lot more money.

Although no one is officially keeping count, by the end of the day I'm sure that Eliza has spent more than $10,000 and I am astounded. Even Taylor seems a little surprised, although she doesn't say much. I sense that she knows better.

Now I realize that Eliza's family is very wealthy, but I still don't get that kind of spending. And for what? A few pieces of clothing and accessories that will probably be out of style next year—at least in some circles. And, excuse me, but I think an African village could eat well for several years on what Miss Wilton spent today. Although I won't make a scene, I suddenly find this whole thing rather disturbing.

Equally unsettling is the way Eliza and Paige appear to be stuck in this ridiculous competition. At the last boutique, Christian Dior, they actually get into a squabble over a white patent belt that Paige asked the clerk to set aside for her to purchase—but while Paige is trying on a suede jacket, Eliza sneaks the belt from behind the counter and buys it from another sales person.

"That's my belt," Paige points out as she sees the unwary sales girl wrapping it in tissue.

"I just bought it," Eliza smugly tells her.

"But I had set it aside," Paige nods to the other clerk, speaking in French, and the clerk confirms this and even attempts to take it away from the other sales girl.

"I've already paid for it." Eliza holds up her American Express card, which I'm surprised hasn't melted after all the action it's seen today.

"I'm sure they can credit it back to—"

"I don't want them to credit it back." Eliza gives Paige a defiant look and Paige looks momentarily stymied.

Now, while Fran and the crew and even Taylor seem

somewhat amused by all this, I think Eliza is being more than a little rude. And I'm halfway tempted to say so. But fortunately, and probably because cameras are still running, Paige quickly recovers and even manages to make light of it.

"Oh, well, you know what they say," she quietly tells the cameras. "Imitation is the sincerest form of flattery. I should feel honored that Eliza Wilton wants what I want so badly she practically has to steal it from me." She laughs.

But it doesn't seem that funny when Eliza continues her attempts to upstage Paige. It's almost as if she thinks our show is up for grabs and whoever gets the most airtime wins. Thankfully there is such a thing as editing and I'm sure that much of Eliza's grasping will end up on the cutting room floor. Yet even as Paige is trying to wrap it up with her best foot forward line, pointing to her shoes, which naturally are Louboutins, Eliza interrupts with what I'm sure she thinks is a witty comment as she describes her own shoes. But with cameras still rolling, no one sees the humor and JJ lets out a groan as Fran just shakes her head. The crew is worn out and ready to call it a day, and Eliza is still trying to be clever.

Of course this simply results in a retake. I can tell that Paige is getting fed up too, although she manages to keep her humor intact, delivers her final lines, and then the cameras shut down. At this juncture Paige gives Eliza a chilly smile and says that we'll see them at Dylan's show tomorrow before she walks off to join Fran—as in, *enough is enough!*

Trying to sound more congenial than I feel, I also tell Taylor and Eliza good-bye. Eliza acts slightly affronted as she picks up her bags and walks away. Taylor laughs, "It's always interesting to witness someone's true colors, especially on film." JJ chuckles as he puts his camera back into its case, but I notice that he and Taylor exchange glances. I'm relieved to know that I'm not the only one who gets put out at Eliza's games.

And Taylor is right. It is interesting to see how some people act when they're in the limelight. Not to mention revealing. I just hope that our viewers can see beyond the façade of fashion and the influence of money and other superficialities ... and figure out for themselves what's really important.

Chapter
11

It's reassuring to hear that Blake feels much better now. I have a nice long chat with him on Thursday night and he seems back to his old cheerful self. I even risk telling him about my dinner out with Gabin, even though I'm careful to call it an "undate." To my relief, Blake does not sound jealous. And, really, why should he be?

On Friday morning we visit *Vogue Paris* and, although Paige does her best to be charming and witty and smart, they seem unilaterally unimpressed. The interview wraps up much sooner than expected and it feels as if they can't wait to be rid of us.

"*Ne permettez pas à la porte de vous frapper sur la voie dehors,*" Paige says as we walk to the car.

"Huh?" I ask.

"Don't let the door hit you on your way out," Fran translates for me, then laughs.

Paige laughs too, although I can tell by her creased forehead that she does not find this funny. I feel for her. She was really trying in there.

"That's how it goes sometimes," Fran says as we climb back in the car. "You can't let it get to you."

But it's already gotten to her. I can tell she's seriously bummed. I know that she had great expectations for *Vogue Paris*. Expectations that fell flatter than a crepe.

"Was it something I said?" she asks both of us. "Do you think I offended someone?"

"I have no idea," I admit. "I honestly thought you were doing great."

"Maybe they were having a bad publishing day," Fran tells her.

"Yeah," I agree. "Or maybe someone's dog died."

"Or maybe some valuable client canceled all their ad space in next month's issue," Fran suggests.

"Or maybe someone lost a great cover photo," I try.

"Okay, okay." Paige holds up her hands. "Maybe you're right. Maybe they were just having a bad day."

"So, let's move on and let it go," Fran advises her. "We still have the Dylan Marceau show this afternoon."

"And you've been looking forward to that," I remind her.

"Except that Eliza Wilton is going to be there." She frowns. "Can you try to keep her away from me, Fran?"

Fran chuckles. "I'm not making any promises. Besides, you know how we feel about controversy in reality TV."

Paige rolls her eyes. "Yeah, yeah, the viewers will eat it up."

"Put the candies where the kiddies can reach them." I sarcastically repeat one of Helen Hudson's favorite adages. It means we should give the audience what they want even if it's not that good for them.

"So ... did you girls notice the sparks between JJ and Taylor yesterday?" Fran asks nonchalantly.

"Sparks as in romance?" Paige questions.

Fran nods.

"Seriously?" I try to remember when I saw them looking at each other.

"I first noticed JJ was sticking pretty close to Taylor when you were in Gucci. I couldn't blame him though." Fran talks as she checks phone messages. "That girl is so gorgeous. No wonder Dylan Marceau loves having her model for him."

"But what makes you think sparks?" I ask curiously. "Was it mutual? Was Taylor looking back?"

"Oh, yeah." Fran nods. "She was subtle about it, but she was definitely looking—maybe even flirting."

"Well, JJ's a good guy. And nice looking too," Paige says. "How old is he anyway?"

"I'm not sure. Mid twenties."

"But he has a girlfriend," I point out. I happen to know things like this since I hang with the camera crew so much.

"*Had* a girlfriend," Fran corrects me. "They broke up a few weeks ago."

"Oh." I nod. "But it's not like JJ and Taylor would get serious. They live on different sides of the country."

Fran laughs. "I wasn't suggesting they're about to get married, Erin. I merely mentioned that there seemed to be some electricity going on between them. But enough of that." Fran begins to go over the plan for our afternoon event—or what we've dubbed *the Dylan Marceau French Debut*. She goes over her notes and although it really doesn't sound much different than the way we've covered fashion shows in the past, I listen.

Fortunately, I'll be on camera crew this time so most of the pressure is off. Maybe I'll catch some sparks flying between JJ and Taylor—that might be fun to get on tape and I'm sure our viewers would enjoy it. And, really, a relationship between those two might even make sense, because they're both genuinely nice people.

"And after the show," Fran is continuing, "we'll head back to the hotel for a little rest. Then Luis and Shauna will come over around six to do hair and makeup."

"Why?" I ask, wondering if I missed something.

"The *after show*," Paige informs me. "Remember?"

I shrug. Truthfully, I don't remember. "Dylan's after show?"

"Of course. It sounds like he's invited a number of people in the fashion industry to this event." Fran rattles off some names. "I think that's very smart on Dylan's part."

"And it won't hurt him to have us there too," Paige points out.

So it's going to be a long night, and I'm already feeling a little tired after a fairly long week. "What about the weekend?" I ask. "Do we get any time off for good behavior?"

Fran laughs. "As a matter of fact, you do. Saturday and Sunday are completely free."

"Don't you ever look at the schedule?" Paige asks.

"Sure," I say. "But it's not like I memorize it."

"And thanks to a cancellation on Monday, you can have a three-day weekend. We don't have another booking until Tuesday afternoon."

"Wow ... three and half days to do whatever." I begin to mentally list the places I still haven't seen, like the Louvre and Notre Dame and Sacre Coeur.

Due to some confusion in scheduling, we arrive for Dylan's show much earlier than necessary. This gives us a whole extra hour before our camera crew arrives. But Heather, one of

Dylan's assistants, is playing host and doesn't even seem to mind that we're early.

"What a beautiful location," Paige says as Heather gives us a quick tour of what once was a palatial estate but is now restored into an events center. Fortunately I brought both my digital and video cameras, and right now I'm taping our tour with Paige and Heather's commentary because Fran thinks we might be able to use some of it for the show. "Wouldn't it be a great spot for a wedding?"

"One of Dylan's models helped us get this place," Heather explains. "Her mother has a home in Southern France and she seems to know everyone who is anyone."

"Let me guess ..." Paige fakes a thoughtful expression. "Would that be Eliza Wilton by any chance?"

"How did you know?" Heather asks.

"We went shopping with Eliza and Taylor yesterday," Paige explains. "We actually met them in New York last month." Just then we spot Dylan, looking dapper and stylish in a white linen suit, hurrying through the gardens toward us. Fortunately I manage to get most of this on tape. With what looks to be a genuinely happy smile, he takes both of Paige's hands and greets her like his long-lost love.

"It's so wonderful to see you again," he tells her.

"*Dylan Marceau*," she says for the sake of my camera. "Today is your big day!"

He beams at her. "Excitement is in the air."

"And I can't believe you're taking time out of your busy schedule to say hello to us." She turns to my camera. "Does he look nervous to you?" Then back to Dylan. "Actually you look great, Dylan. And you seem cool as a cucumber."

Dylan laughs. "Then I'm a better actor than I thought."

"This is a huge event for you," Paige says with enthusiasm. "Returning to the home of your ancestors as one of the latest, greatest American fashion designers. It must be wonderful. I know you're busy and we don't want to take too much of your time, but our viewers would love to hear how you're feeling right now, Dylan."

"Well . . . I'm excited and nervous. Confident and worried. Ecstatic and anxious." He chuckles. "I am a regular dichotomy of emotion." He leans over and kisses Paige on the cheek. "But I feel much better knowing you are here, Paige Forrester. Thank you for sharing in this moment with me."

Paige actually blushes—ever so slightly. *"Thank you!"*

"And now I must run, darling. See you at the after party?"

"I wouldn't miss it," she calls as he heads back through the lush gardens. She turns back to me, smiling like a conspirator for the sake of her viewers. "Isn't it amazing to be privy to the private moments of a great designer like Dylan Marceau—just on the cusp of international fame? Imagine how it would feel to be an American of French descent, to be making your own mark in an arena where Parisians rule, standing up in front of everyone to display your own original designs— and knowing that fashion critics and harsh reviewers will be seated amongst your audience." She shudders dramatically. "I'm not sure I could take the pressure, but I can't wait to see how this turns out."

I smile at the irony as I continue shooting. I know full well that Paige can and does take the pressure every time she steps into center stage on our show. With confidence she lays her style sense and fashion opinions on the line almost every time she opens her mouth—at least when cameras are rolling. And, lucky for her, fans seem to respect her. According to Fran,

Paige's ratings are steadily climbing. We just learned that Japan is looking into syndicating our show, and some of the European markets are interested as well.

"Do you want to get some of the behind-the-scenes shots with the models?" Heather offers. "Dylan said it was okay."

"That would be awesome," Paige tells her. We follow Heather into a large room being used as the changing and staging area which is not nearly as chaotic as it will likely become in the next hour. While there are some last-minute alterations and fittings going on, it's relatively calm. Or maybe it's just the calm before the storm. Hopefully it will go well for Dylan today. As I remember the frosty reception we got at *Vogue Paris* this morning, I know that there's no way to predict how the French couture world will receive Dylan's fall lineup.

I also overheard Paige telling Fran that some fashion icons had warned Dylan not to even make this attempt. Some said that he was too new, too young, and that his clothes, along with his reputation, would be chewed up and spit out by the French elite. For Dylan's sake I hope and pray they are wrong. Because I've met a lot of designers and people involved in fashion and Dylan is right amongst the top of my favorites list. I'd hate to see him hurt.

Paige manages to snag some interviews with some of the models, although language is a challenge since some of them are from countries besides France. Then just as more models arrive and things begin to speed up—getting louder and busier—our crew arrives. Fran puts them to work filming behind the scenes with models and then, as guests arrive, taping whatever off-the-cuff interviews Paige is able to capture. With some of the snootier French critics it's a challenge, and this worries me even more.

Suddenly everyone is seated, the lights are turned down low, and it's show time. Camera flashes are banned until after the show, and so I simply sit next to Paige and watch as model after model struts forward—much like New York Fashion Week, but even better. Yet the audience seems unresponsive. Even when Dylan's star—Taylor Mitchell—struts the runway, there's not the usual rush of excitement. Despite Paige's and my attempts to clap and generate enthusiasm, it feels as if almost everyone else is asleep.

Finally the show ends and there is polite applause. Feeling worried for Dylan's sake, I rejoin the camera crew and using my digital with a flash, I continue to shoot photos of the models. Of course, Eliza and Taylor are among them, and although I don't want to be too obvious, I don't go out of my way to shoot Eliza. For two reasons: One, I'm still a little irked with her, and two, she's not nearly as interesting as the other models.

Because there is no ovation, Dylan never makes another appearance and I feel even worse as I imagine him hiding in the back somewhere, feeling like a failure. I wish there was something we could do—some way to help. Then I notice that Paige is still conducting interviews with our camera guys still filming her, and I decide to go over and see what's happening.

To my surprise the audience's reaction is a bit warmer than I realized. As I pull out my video camera, I'm able to catch some of it on tape. To my huge relief, Paige is getting them to comment on Dylan's line and the comments are really rather positive. I can tell that Paige is kind of fishing for some compliments as she compares Dylan's work to some of the more classic French designers, playing the ancestor card, and pointing out how France really is the gold standard of fashion and style. Naturally, this pleases them and they warm up even more.

And, although Paige is using her charm and knowledge to influence them, I'm not stupid. I happen to know that Parisians can be very stubborn about style. If they don't like something there's no way you can convince them they do. If anything, Paige is simply helping them to admit that Dylan is a good designer. "Il est l'un de leurs propres" she says more than once. *One of their own.*

By the time we finish up shooting, I think they agree. Dylan Marceau really is one of their own. Unfortunately, Heather has looked everywhere and Dylan is nowhere to be found, so he can't enjoy this. Heather thanks Paige over and over and promises to relay this good news to Dylan.

"Poor Dylan," Paige says as we're riding back to the hotel. "He must've been devastated."

"I've never seen a chillier audience," Fran admits. "I honestly thought Dylan's design career was over."

"Me too," I say. "I was actually praying for him."

"Hopefully he'll feel better about all this in time for the after party," Paige says. "Because he really should be celebrating tonight. Despite how things looked, I think he'll be pleased when he sees the reviews. At least I hope so." She releases a nervous sigh.

"Who knew that the French would be such a tough crowd?" I shake my head. "It reminds me of a place in the Bible where Jesus mentions about how he's not accepted in his hometown. I wonder if that's kind of how Dylan felt today."

Neither of them responds and I suspect either they don't get it ... or maybe I made them uncomfortable. I really do think there's a similarity, and I think it must hurt a lot when the people you expect to accept you don't.

We get back to the hotel in time for a short nap before Luis and Shauna arrive to help with our hair and makeup. As Shauna works on me, she commiserates over the Dylan dilemma.

"Paige told me all about it," she says. "These French people can be so snooty."

"Oh, I don't know," I say in defense. "I've met some very nice ones. I think they're not that different from Americans. Some can be arrogant, others can be sweet." Of course, I'm thinking of Gabin. He really is a great guy. But just thinking about him makes me think about Blake ... and then Lionel. I cannot believe I am thinking about three guys. What is going on with me?

"Maybe ... but that day we were at Dominique's for your makeovers, I felt the snub from several of the employees."

"Maybe they were intimidated by you and Luis," I point out. "You probably have more experience than some. And you've worked on celebrities." I kind of laugh. "Not me. But I've heard Fran mention some names."

"Hey, I'd rather work on you than a lot of celebs."

"So, see, Americans can be snooty too."

She nods as she fluffs a blush brush. "I guess you're right."

I determine to use today's experience as a reminder. Every country has its own selection of snobs and every-day good people. Who knows, maybe people simply reflect what they think we're giving to them. Anyway, it makes me

determined to sport a better attitude. I guess I should take
lessons from my sister because when it comes to gracious-
ness, she's much more of a natural than I am. Seriously, I can
be such a whiner sometimes. I decide I will definitely try
harder ... even with snooty people like Eliza Wilton. God
help me. Because, really, God is the only one who can help
me to love someone like that.

Chapter
12

Paige decides she wants to arrive fashionably late to Dylan's after party and since that means we get a little more time to linger over dinner and visit with the crew, I don't mind a bit. It turns out that Fran's hunch about JJ being into Taylor was spot on. When Paige mentions Taylor's name, it seems to be written all over JJ's face that the poor guy is smitten with her. Alistair gets him to admit it, and after we all soundly tease him about his little infatuation, JJ begs us to keep it under our hats. For his sake, I will. I can't make any promises for my sister though, because on our way over to the party, she acts almost as if she plans to play Cupid tonight. Poor JJ.

"Do you girls have any plans for what you're going to do with your three and a half days off?" Fran asks absently as she checks her phone for messages.

"You mean besides shop?" Paige answers as she opens her phone to check for messages.

"I'd like to see the Louvre," I admit. "And some of the other sites."

"Hey, here's good news from Benjamin," Paige announces.

"Mia's family has settled out of court. And for only about half of what his attorney was predicting."

"That was lucky," Fran says.

"The condition was that he has to make a final appearance on *Malibu Beach*," Paige continues to read. "And confess that he was an idiot to drink and drive, and encourage fans to learn from this hard lesson."

"That seems like a step in the right direction," I say as I turn on my phone. This is a good time of day (night here and morning at home) to catch up on emails and texts. I see a similar message from Blake, explaining the settlement and that Benjamin not only agreed to it, but scheduled the shoot segment today. And that he'd invited Blake to join him for moral support. I report this news to Paige.

"Text Blake back and thank him for me," Paige tells me. "I owe that boy."

"Don't you mean Benjamin owes him?" I point out.

"Yes, of course. But it takes such a load off knowing that Blake is being a good friend. You know how guilty I've felt about kind of abandoning Benjamin?"

"It's not like you had much choice," Fran tells her. "All things considered, Benjamin was lucky you'd even speak to him after all that."

I'm texting Blake now, repeating Paige's thanks and telling him about the party we're headed to. I mention how Dylan is probably a little blue, but that I think Paige will cheer him up. I finish with "more tomorrow" and sign off.

"This looks like the place," Fran announces as our driver pulls to a stop. "Now the plan is to only have the crew there for about half an hour," she tells Paige. "It was very generous of Dylan to allow that much."

"Hey, it's publicity," I remind her.

She winks at me. "I know it. But the day will come when the boy will be so famous he'll turn away all forms of press at events like this."

"Even us?" Paige makes a wounded face.

Fran laughs. "Probably not you, dear. I have a feeling Dylan will always have a soft spot for you."

But when we get up to the penthouse where the party should be in full swing, there is an odd sort of quiet in the room. Sure, there's music playing, but the guests seem rather subdued. We soon learn that Dylan hasn't shown up yet.

"He took off right after the show," Taylor explains when she and Eliza come over to join us. "Everyone thinks it's because he was so bummed by the response."

"You mean lack of response," Eliza adds.

"Has anyone tried to call him?" Paige asks.

"Eliza just tried," Taylor says. "Went straight to voicemail."

Paige whips out her phone. "Well, maybe I'll try to call him."

"It won't do any good," Eliza says glumly.

We all wait, with cameras still running, and the next thing we know Paige is bubbling away, telling him what a success the show was and how she's here at the after party and asking where he is. It appears she's leaving a message, but then she pauses and nods like she's listening, and it seems as if Dylan is on the other end.

Everyone presses a little closer to Paige, as if they want to hear what he's saying.

"No, Dylan, I'm not just saying that. It's true. I talked to lots of people afterward. If you don't believe me, you can watch it on tape. It just took people a bit to warm up. And the more we chatted, the more it became obvious that they really liked you. Hey, some of them really loved you. If you come to-night, you can hear some of this from their very own mouths. Or else you will read about it in the papers tomorrow and the magazines when they come out." She pauses again. "I'm totally serious, Dylan. If you don't get over here in the next ten minutes, I will take my crew and leave." Another pause. "Yes, I would be devastated too, darling. *Voir-vous bientôt!*" She hangs up and smiles to the cameras. "The party boy will be here shortly."

Naturally, she has gotten everyone's attention. She takes turns chatting with everyone and anyone while the cameras are rolling, and I can tell we're going to have some good out-takes from this evening. When Dylan arrives, he rushes di-rectly to Paige as if she's his personal savior, and, swooping her into his arms, he plants a kiss right on her lips. Of course, this too is caught by the cameras and a lot of onlookers actu-ally clap and laugh and even cheer. Suddenly this previously lackluster party swings into high gear.

For the next half hour or so, Dylan, with Paige at his side, greets his other guests and receives their compliments and makes his apologies. I feel a little unnecessary, and since my feet are already screaming from the Christian Louboutins that Paige loaned me, I find a quiet table and just sit and wait. To my surprise, Eliza eventually joins me. She's very quiet and I can tell she's feeling bummed over something. Thinking she's still worried about Dylan, I try to reassure her that the worst is over.

"Yes, I'm sure it seems that way." She looks away, as if she wants someone more interesting to talk to. Instead of feeling offended, I remember my earlier resolve to be nicer. Plus, she's the one who came to sit by me.

"That was sure a beautiful place to have Dylan's show," I tell her. "I heard you had something to do with that."

She brightens. "Yes. Actually my mother found it. And a number of my mother's friends were there today too."

"Was that fun for them to see you on the runway?" I ask. "I'll bet your mother was proud."

She shrugs. "My mother isn't really into any of this. She thinks I'm just going through a phase."

I can't help but think her mother must be right. After all, most models have the shelf life of, say, a tomato. But I'm so not going there. Instead, I compliment her on her runway expertise. "I actually had to model once," I confess. "I was pretty bad."

"Well, it's not easy," she confides. "I'll never be as good as Taylor." She frowns. "No one is as good as Taylor."

"She does make it look easy."

"Yes, but it's not easy."

"Then why do you want to do it?" I ask. I still remember the night in New York when she and Taylor and some friends got into it one night — the discussion over modeling and why someone as wealthy as Eliza would invest so much energy into it. But I don't recall her reasoning.

"I don't know." She sighs. "I guess I'm just a glutton for punishment."

This makes me laugh and Taylor comes our way. "Hey, girls," she says as she pulls out a chair. "What's so funny?" I fill her in on our conversation, which doesn't seem so funny anymore.

Taylor leans toward me, lowering her voice. "So, Erin, tell me about your camera guy."

I grin knowingly. "You mean JJ?"

She just nods, and I laugh.

"What is it?" Eliza demands. "What's the joke?"

I nod over to where JJ and Alistair are still trailing Paige and Dylan. "See the dark-haired camera guy, the younger one?" I tell her.

Eliza nods. "Oh, yeah, I noticed him before. He's really good-looking."

"He thinks Taylor's good-looking too."

"He's also pretty nice," Taylor says. "Anyway, he seems to be. Not that I really know him."

"Well, he made us promise not to say anything." I chuckle. "But it's not like I brought it up."

"So what did he say?" Taylor asks with a calm sort of interest.

"Just that he'd like to get to know you."

She smiles.

"And guess what?" I tell her. "Our show is taking three and a half days off. We don't go back to recording until Tuesday afternoon. So we'll all be hanging out in the city with time to spare—if you know what I mean."

Taylor makes a face then turns to Eliza. "We promised your mom we'd come visit this weekend."

"Her benefit fashion show's on Monday," Eliza reminds her. "You can't back out now."

"A fashion show?" I venture. "Anything our TV show would be interested in?"

"It's pretty small potatoes and I doubt—" Taylor stops then turns to Eliza. "Hey, why don't we invite everyone down there too?"

"Oh, I don't know." Eliza frowns. "I seriously doubt my mom will want her little soiree to turn into a reality show."

Taylor nods. "Yes ... you're probably right."

Just then Paige and Dylan come over to our table, trailed by the camera crew. "So this is where the cool kids' table is." Paige teases as she sits next to me.

Dylan takes a chair next to Eliza then lets out what sounds like a huge sigh of relief. "Ah, to be among real friends."

Eliza turns to him. "I take it you're feeling a little better about your show now, Dylan?"

He reaches for her hand and gives it a squeeze. "Yes, dear. Much better. Thanks for asking."

Eliza's face lights up then clouds over slightly. "But why didn't you believe me when I called and left a message earlier?"

"I don't know." He shakes his head. "I was so down. I listened to a few messages and figured everyone was trying to cheer me up. I just knew I was a colossal flop and I was so embarrassed I didn't know what to do. I wanted to tuck my tail between my legs and run. And yet I was too humiliated to even go back to New York. I wanted to disappear."

"Where did you go?" Taylor asks.

"Just down the street," he admits. "A little bistro near where my grandmother used to live. I thought I'd find comfort there. Instead, I just got bluer and bluer. I kept thinking of all the money I'd wasted on this foolish little venture and how people had advised against it. And how much I'd owe my creditors and whether or not my company could survive it ... or if my career could survive it." He pauses to look across the table to Paige. "Thankfully, I was wrong."

We all chat a bit more about Dylan's show and the initial reaction and how the French can take a bit to warm up. Then Fran, who's been hovering nearby, begins motioning to the camera crew that it's time to shut it down. But I can tell Taylor is still wishing for an opportunity to get better acquainted with JJ, and I know he feels the same. So with no real plan in mind, I jump in.

"You know Taylor and Eliza are going down to her parents' chateau and vineyard in Southern France tomorrow," I begin slowly. "I've heard it's really pretty down there ..." I direct this to Paige. "I wonder if there might be some things we could shoot down there for our show."

Paige looks skeptical. "Our show's about fashion, Erin. I don't really see the connection."

"Besides," Dylan speaks up, "I promised Paige that I'd show her the Parisian sites for the next few days while you girls are having your little sabbatical."

I look directly at our camera guys, specifically JJ, as in *hint-hint.* "Well, you guys have time off too," I say. "Maybe you'll want to go down there and get some extra footage anyway. I'll bet you could get some good photos of the French countryside to use as filler on the show." Okay, I know this is ridiculous since filler is usually fashion shots, but hey, I'm trying. And I can tell that JJ is appreciative.

Fran gets this funny little smile and I can tell she gets what I'm attempting. "You know, that's not a bad idea," she says. Although JJ looks a little embarrassed, I can see that he's pleased too. He nods.

"I'm sure it's really photogenic down there," he says to Fran. "Erin might be right. We could probably use some filler shots."

"It's really gorgeous country there," Taylor says temptingly. "Especially this time of year when everything is in bloom. I'll even be taking a camera myself."

"Well, it's up to you guys," Fran tells JJ and Alistair, but already they're smiling like it's a done deal. "Just keep track of your mileage and make sure you make it back by noon on Tuesday."

Paige grins at the camera guys. "And I can't say I'll miss you boys for a few days. It'll be seriously fun to trek around Paris without having my personal paparazzi on our heels."

"I'm with you," Dylan agrees. "And I'm a guy who almost never says no to publicity ops."

"Hey, I have an idea," Eliza says suddenly. "Why don't *you all* come down to the chateau for the weekend?"

Paige holds up her hand. "Oh, but I don't think we—"

"No, it would be great to have everyone there. And I'm sure you'd love it," Eliza continues with her eyes fixed on Dylan. "There's plenty of room for everyone. Your crew could shoot whatever they like, Paige. Dylan might even loan some of his fall line of designs for my mother's little benefit fashion show. Lots of her rich and influential friends will be there, Dylan. You could do some serious schmoozing, get some publicity, and still have some fun."

"There's a fashion show?" Paige asks with interest.

"Just a small private affair that Taylor and I offered to model for, but I might be able to talk Mommy into opening it up to your cameras too. After all, it's for charity—the more the merrier."

I can't say anything, but methinks this girl is trying too hard. She's too eager. I'm pretty sure it's because of Dylan.

"You're sure your parents won't mind if we crash in on them?" Fran asks with interest.

"Actually, my father's not even there. Mommy won't even get back from her Rome trip until Sunday night. And, trust me, there's plenty of room."

"That's true," Taylor confirms. "I've been there and the place is huge. It used to be a castle. And the food is amazing."

"It sounds enchanting," Fran says with raised brows. "And a small private French fashion show could be quite interesting for *On the Runway* ... that is, if your mother doesn't mind."

Eliza looks directly at Dylan. "I think if Dylan is willing to share some of his fall lineup, my mother should be willing to share her show."

"Oh, you will, won't you, Dylan?" Paige asks with enthusiasm.

Dylan looks slightly hesitant. Then he agrees. "Like I said, I'm a fool for publicity. Sure, why not."

But as I'm watching Eliza watch Dylan like a hungry cat eyes a parakeet, I can think of some reasons why not. I saw Eliza's initial reluctance to the whole idea when I suggested it. In fact, it was only when Paige announced that she and Dylan would spend time together in Paris this weekend that Eliza jumped onto this weekend-party bandwagon.

It's not like I can put the brakes on it, but suddenly I'm feeling concerned for my oblivious sister. Not to mention slightly guilty for having brought up this idea in the first place. Hopefully I'm just being paranoid. On the other hand, if it all blows up, I'll probably be the one to blame.

Chapter
13

"Someone's looking for you, Erin," *Heather* whispers into my ear just as I'm about to suggest it's time for Paige and me to head back to our hotel. Fran left Dylan's after party a couple hours ago with the excuse that she needed to contact Leah and start arranging travel plans for our weekend at the chateau.

"Who?" I ask Heather.

She smiles slyly. "A handsome young man named Gabin. His invitation was through Hermès. Does that ring a bell?"

"He's here?"

"Over by the door. Please, make him feel welcome ... if you don't mind. Dylan's trying to cultivate good relationships within the French design world. As you know, it's not easy."

"No problem," I tell her. "Gabin is a friend." I make my way through the crowd to find him. He seems happy to see me and we embrace. I invite him to come over and sit with Dylan and our friends.

"If it is no trouble," he says politely.

"Dylan would love to meet you." I take his hand and lead him over. Dylan seems genuinely pleased to meet Gabin and they strike up quite a conversation. In a way I suppose they are competitors, but Gabin acts like a perfect gentleman and expresses his regrets after Dylan confesses that he's afraid his show bombed today.

"You know the French," Gabin tells him in careful English. "One day we are chilly, and then voila, we become warm. Do not be too hard on yourself."

Suddenly I realize how late it is, and how tired I am, so I nudge Paige. "Do you think we should call it a night?" I ask hopefully. "Especially since we'll need to pack and get ready to leave in the morning."

Gabin turns to me with concerned eyes. "You are leaving? So soon?"

Dylan explains our weekend travel plans, then turns to Eliza with a broad smile. "Sweet Eliza," he says warmly. "What do you think?"

She smiles back at him. "I would love to have Gabin join us for the weekend."

Gabin looks pleased to have been included and says he'd be delighted to come.

"Eliza and I are traveling by train," Taylor tells everyone, including JJ, who's sitting next to her. "That's because I happen to love trains. If anyone else wants to tag along, our departure is at nine fifteen in the morning. You might need to call ahead to reserve your tickets."

"There are lots of trains after that," Eliza explains. "But we wanted to be there by noon."

"Going by train sounds fun," Paige says to me. "Do you think Fran would mind?"

"Let's find out." I reach for my phone. As I press speed dial I'm thinking of the great photo ops I'll have along the way. Fortunately Fran is okay with it. "But if you don't mind, I'll go in the town car and work along the way. You girls can pack up what you want to take down there—since our rooms here are paid for there's no need to pack it all up. Leave your bags with the concierge in the lobby and I'll have our driver load them up before I go."

"That sounds great," I tell her. "Traveling light."

Fran offers to arrange for our train tickets and by the time I hang up, it seems to be settled. "It looks like Paige and I will be going by train as well," I announce.

Dylan already has Heather busily making arrangements for him and his new best buddy Gabin. I can't help chuckling at how these guys are hitting it off. It even looks like JJ is going to try to make the train as well.

"If no one minds, I can shoot some film along the way," he quietly tells Paige and me. She just laughs then nods, but I can tell that, like me, she's thinking his camera will be primarily aimed at Taylor. Even so, that would probably make for some good footage. Why wouldn't our fans want to watch a beautiful fashion model taking the train to Bordeaux in the springtime?

Finally I insist we call it a night. "Morning is going to come early," I point out to Paige, and she reluctantly agrees to leave the party.

"May I offer you and Paige a ride?" Gabin asks slowly and carefully, like he's practicing.

"Wonderful," Paige tells him. "Then we won't have to wait for a taxi."

As Gabin drives us to our hotel, he explains how he's

been working hard on his English skills. "In Bordeaux will be—how you say—a good *pratique* ... language *éducation* for me."

At the hotel we thank him for the ride. "*Voyez-vous le matin*," I call.

"Yes." He pauses as if he's thinking hard. "See you the morning."

"He's sweet," Paige says as we ride the elevator up. "And Dylan was so pleased that you introduced them."

"They seemed to have hit it off," I say as we get out.

"And Gabin seems to have his eye on you," she tells me, pulling out her room key.

I consider protesting and making my usual disclaimers, but the truth is I'm too tired. I just nod as I dig for my key and tell Paige I'll see her in the morning. Our plan is to leave the hotel around eight.

Once I'm in my room, I realize I need to pack for three days and I honestly have no idea what one takes to a chateau in Bordeaux. I have a feeling my usual casual clothing might not be suitable, so I make sure to put in some other things too. Finally too tired to think, I decide I'll entrust the rest of my wardrobe challenges to my sister. If she doesn't like how I look, I'm sure she'll jump in and help me.

"You're wearing *that?*" Paige lifts up her Gucci sunglasses to frown at me once we're out on the sidewalk.

"What?" I look down at my hastily assembled ensemble. I thought Paige would appreciate that I wore a skirt. Okay, it's not French, but it's Ralph Lauren. A neat little khaki number, topped with a white Lauren polo shirt.

Her mouth twists to one side. "Where did you get that cardigan?"

"I found it in a little retro shop down the street."

She plucks at the loose cuff and shakes her head. "Well, you should've left it there. Did you not notice it's way too big for you?"

"But it's kind of cool today," I point to the cloudy sky. "And it's a warm sweater."

"Well, it will be warmer down in Bordeaux." She shakes her head as she grabs me by the arm. "Lose the sweater, Erin."

"There's our taxi, we should — "

She waves at the driver, yelling in French that we'll be right back. Once we're in the lobby, she heads straight for one of her many pieces of luggage that Fran will bring in the town car with her. She unzips the bag and digs until she finds another sweater. "Here." She hands the navy cardigan to me. "This should be warm enough."

"Thanks." I remove my sweater and stuff it into my duffle bag then pull on the cardigan — a zippered cashmere, also a Ralph Lauren, and it actually feels pretty good.

"Much better," she says as we hurry out to the taxi.

On the way to the train station, Paige seems unusually quiet. Finally, I can't stand it. "Is something wrong?" I ask her. "I mean, did I do something or was the sweater really that bad or ..." I look down at my Birkin bag. Surely she's not still upset about that.

She blinks. "No, no, you didn't do anything, Erin. Sorry, I probably seem like a grump."

"What's up?"

She adjusts the front of her jacket, a pale pink classic, probably Chanel, then smoothes her pants, which are white and perfect-looking. Paige is the only person I know who can wear white pants on a train trip and probably arrive at her destination looking just as perfect as she does now. Her Pepto-Bismol pumps match her Kelly bag, and she has a pink and blue scarf that is very Grace Kelly-ish. "I need to just let it go."

"What?" I persist.

"Benjamin."

"Huh?"

"Oh, we've been texting and, naturally, I told him about our trip to Bordeaux before I went to bed last night. Just making small talk. And I mentioned how Dylan Marceau is being very attentive. And when I read Ben's text this morning, actually several of them, I can tell he's feeling bad. He thinks he's losing me." She sighs and shakes her head.

"Losing you?" I frown. "I didn't think you guys were really together, Paige."

"We're not. Not really. Ben knows this, and yet he keeps holding on."

"Oh."

"But I'm not going to think about it."

"You mean until you get the next text from him."

She gives me a half smile. "The problem is I still like him, Erin."

"Like him as in really like him, or just like him as a friend?"

She shrugs. "I'm not sure."

"How about Dylan?" I ask out of genuine curiosity.

"What do you mean?"

"Do you like him?"

"Of course. Dylan is a sweetheart. What's not to like?"

"You know what I mean, Paige. Dylan is into you. It's obvious. Do you feel the same?"

She holds up her hands in frustration. "I don't really know how I feel. Mostly I want to be free and just enjoy the moment ... and the person I'm with. The show takes up so much time and energy—it's not like I can even have a serious relationship right now. I wish everyone could get that."

I nod. "I get that."

"Yeah. It's kind of like that with you too, isn't it?" She smiles. "*Vives et laissé vivre.*"

"Absolutely." I nod. "*Live and let live.*"

"Let's do that then. The next few days we just relax and have fun. Okay?"

"While we're on the subject of fun," I begin cautiously, "I know that Eliza's parents' chateau is part of a vineyard and I assume the wine will flow freely down there."

Paige waves her hand. "Don't worry about me, Erin. A glass with a meal is the most I'll be consuming."

"But what if, like in the past, one glass leads to another and—"

"Seriously, Erin. You need to lighten up a little ... and trust me, okay?"

"Okay ..." Still I'm not so sure.

"I mean, this is France after all. Do you know what the legal drinking age is over here?"

"Two?" I tease. I've heard that French children drink wine diluted with water.

She laughs. "No. It's eighteen. And it's acceptable to drink wine at even younger ages, if you're with your family. It's like it's no big deal here. Meanwhile in the good old US of A kids think they're being all rebellious by sneaking alcohol. Over here, it's like why bother?"

I consider this and wonder. She might have a point.

By the time we get to the train station, we realize we'll need to hurry to catch the train. Thankfully, we have no luggage and security goes smoothly, and so we manage to board just minutes before the train pulls out.

"You made it." Dylan gives us both a hug. "We were getting worried, and I was assigned the task to watch for you." He leads us up to the first class car where Gabin, Eliza, and Taylor are already seated.

"Did your camera guys make it?" Taylor asks.

"You mean did JJ make it?" Eliza teases.

"Hopefully they're aboard." Paige reaches for her phone to check. She chats briefly then hangs up. "Their tickets aren't for first class," she tells Taylor.

"But I thought they were going to do some filming," Taylor says. "Maybe we can get them some kind of a press pass or something." She offers to go find out.

Gabin acts as my personal tour guide and, as the train zips along, I attempt to snap some photos as he points out places of interest. Meanwhile, it's obvious that Dylan's main interest lies in Paige. The two of them chat almost nonstop about fashion, France, and our TV show, and his plans to expand his line . . . and occasionally Eliza jumps in. Although Dylan is polite to her, I can tell he wishes he were alone with Paige. And I can tell Eliza knows this—and that she's not happy about it.

"Come with me," Gabin says suddenly. I follow as he leads me through one car and another until finally we get to a car that's mostly windows. I'm able to snag some pretty cool shots, but after awhile, I feel like we should get back. It might be crazy, but I'm worried about leaving Eliza alone with Paige and Dylan. Something about the look in Eliza's eyes felt like a warning to me. I have no doubt that this weekend invitation was Eliza's way of keeping Dylan close by, although I suspect she wishes that my sister was still in Paris. Hopefully Eliza hasn't pushed her off the train by now. Okay, I know that's melodramatic on my part—but I also can tell that Eliza's the kind of girl who goes to extremes to get her own way.

Chapter
14

To my surprise, Eliza is sitting by herself when Gabin and I get back to the first-class car. With her back turned toward us, it looks like she's texting on her phone. Hopefully not making arrangements to have my sister kidnapped or anything.

"Where'd everyone go?" I ask as I sit down.

She turns abruptly, pushing the iPhone into her lap, then shrugs. "I was just wondering that myself."

Gabin and I make attempts at small talk, asking about Eliza's parents' place, but then I notice something strange. Her white iPhone looks exactly like the ones that the studio purchased for Paige and me. That, in itself, isn't so unusual. But her phone, just like Paige's, has a little daisy sticker on the back of it. Paige did that to avoid the confusion of mixing up our phones after we did that once.

"Hey, that's funny," I tell Eliza. "Paige has that same sticker on her phone." I point to the pink daisy.

"This is her phone," Eliza tells me. "She must've dropped it before she left."

"Oh." I reach for it. "I'll take it for her."

Eliza seems reluctant to hand it over, but I don't back off. "Thanks," I say as I drop it into one of the pockets of my bag.

"Nice Birkin bag," Eliza tells me. "I have an orange one."

"*Orange.*" I exchange a glance with Gabin, who looks like he's trying not to chuckle.

"It was *the* color not long ago."

"Erin is more the *classique* type," Gabin says with an appreciative smile. "The black suits her."

Dylan and Paige return and I hand over her phone. "Oh my gosh," she exclaims. "I didn't even know I'd lost it. Thank you!"

"Eliza found it," I tell her. Paige thanks her and slips it into her own bag just as Taylor and the camera guys arrive with their cameras running.

"Now everyone just act normal," Paige directs. "Pretend as if the cameras aren't running."

I try to distract myself from the camera guys by continuing to take photos with my own camera. As I snap one of Eliza and Taylor, I notice how natural Taylor looks although Eliza seems to be posing. I guess that shouldn't surprise me, since she is a model, and, as I recall, this is exactly how she acted when we taped a show in her apartment during Fashion Week.

Just like it did then, it still kind of irks me. And it irks me that it irks me because I know I should get over it. Not only that, I remember my promise to her in New York, and that reminds me that I should really be praying for this girl. Because the more I'm around her, the more I see that her head's a little messed up. I could chalk it up to the poor little rich girl syndrome. But even if that's the case, I know that God loves her as much as anyone else.

As I snap another posed shot of Eliza, I try to see what's behind those pretty blue eyes, perfect nose, and up-tilted chin. What makes this girl tick? I remember the time she fell apart in the women's restroom, sobbing because she wasn't as sought after as Taylor for modeling opportunities. I also remember my challenge to her, suggesting she do something important and valuable with her life—like feed starving children in Africa. Unfortunately, she still seems to be stuck on the fashion track.

The trip to Bordeaux seems to whiz by and as we're getting off the train, Paige and I realize that we didn't make any arrangements for a car to get us from the station to the chateau in Margaux—about a thirty mile trip.

"It might be tight, but you can ride with us," JJ offers as the film crew's van pulls up.

"I have *réservation* for a car," Gabin tells Paige and me. "You can ride with me."

"Some of you can ride with me." Eliza directs this to Dylan. "I had the Fiat dropped off here this morning."

I can see the dismay in Eliza's eyes when it's JJ who, urged by Taylor, accepts the offer of a ride. Meanwhile Gabin, Dylan, Paige, and I go in Gabin's rental car. The plan is for us to follow Eliza, but she drives so fast that Paige begs Gabin to slow down. "We know where Chateau Bertrand is located," she assures him in French. "And we have a map. What does it matter if we're late?"

"And if we slow down we can actually see the countryside," I point out. "Because Taylor wasn't exaggerating. It's gorgeous."

"I can stop," Gabin offers, "if you like to photograph."

I take him up on this offer several times, which slows us down even more. But, really, what's the hurry?

"Maybe we should stop for lunch," Dylan suggests as Gabin comes into a small, quaint town.

"Excellent idea," Gabin tells him. "And we can check the map."

Paige gives Eliza a call, leaving a message that we decided to stop for food. We find a sweet little bistro and as we wait for our orders, the guys consult the map, I switch camera cards, and Paige checks her phone messages. *"What the——?"* she says suddenly.

I look up from my camera to see that my sister looks seriously disturbed. "What's wrong?" I demand. "Is it Mom?"

"No." She shakes her head. "It's Benjamin."

Both guys look up from the map. "Who is Benjamin?" Gabin asks.

"Benjamin Kross," I fill in for him. "Paige's, uh, friend."

Dylan smiles. "And the star of one of America's hottest teen reality TV shows. Well, your show excluded, of course."

"Of course." Paige makes a face.

"So what's up with old Benjamin Kross?" Dylan asks with interest.

"He's lost his mind." Paige holds up her hands helplessly.

"What's going on?" I persist.

"He's coming here."

"Here?" I stare at her. "Here as in France here?"

She just nods.

"Why?"

"To see me."

"I still don't get it," I tell her.

"Neither do I. Somehow he got the impression that I invited him to join us."

"Seriously?"

She looks down at her phone. "Seriously. His first text says: Thanks. I'll call you when I'm in Bordeaux."

"He's coming to Bordeaux?" I'm trying to wrap my head around this. "When does he plan to arrive? We're only here a few days. What time is it there anyway? Isn't it like the middle of the night? How is this even possible?"

"His last text was sent around three in the morning, saying he'd booked a flight that leaves at six forty a.m, and that he was going to take a nap before heading to LAX."

"This is nuts," I tell her.

"He'll arrive in Bordeaux tomorrow morning."

"What made him think you'd invited him?" I ask.

"You mean besides his overactive imagination?"

"He must be in love with you," Gabin offers.

Dylan laughs. "Of course. Why else would someone do something so crazy?"

"Are you in love with him?" Gabin asks Paige.

"No," she says quickly. "Of course not."

Then Dylan tells Gabin about Benjamin's recent scandal and how his costar and former girlfriend died as a result.

Gabin shakes his head. "That is horrible."

Paige tries to tell the story a bit more fairly, explaining about how Mia had been drunk and initiated a fight. Gabin nods, as if he understands. "I hear of this before. Lover disputes in cars ... *dangereux.*"

"And it seems that the court agreed that Benjamin's blood alcohol levels, combined with the other evidence the police gathered, do back up his statement, and show that he was not legally at fault," Paige continues in a weary tone. "Although Mia's family might still push for a civil suit ... but all the charges have been dropped. I guess he feels free to travel."

"I still don't get him inviting himself to Bordeaux," I persist. "Like who does that?" Then I get a flashback—I remember how Eliza had Paige's phone. "Hey, wait a minute," I say suddenly.

"What?" Paige asks.

I remind her about how Eliza supposedly "found" Paige's phone. "When I first came into the car, she appeared to be texting someone," I explain. "At the time I assumed it was her own iPhone. But then I saw the daisy on the back and realized it was your phone."

Paige has her phone out. She's probably checking sent texts and suddenly she lets out a little gasp. "Eliza texted him on my phone," she announces in a stiff voice. "She pretended to be me and invited him to join us at Chateau Bertrand, and she even gave him her phone number so he could call for directions. It was sent at nine forty-two in the morning."

I do the mental math. "That would've been one forty-two am in LA. Pretty late."

"Obviously, Ben was still up." Paige looks at me with troubled eyes.

"Why would Eliza invite this Benjamin?" Gabin asks.

"Maybe because she wants to meet a celebrity?" suggests Dylan.

Just then our lunch arrives. I exchange glances with Paige, then look over at Dylan, hoping she'll get my hint and that I can fill her in later. So even though Eliza didn't push my sister off the train, it looks like she'd like to throw her under one before our visit to Chateau Bertrand is over.

After lunch, Paige and I go to the restroom and I explain my theory. But she's not buying it. "That seems kind of crazy," she tells me as she washes her hands. "It's possible that Dylan nailed it when he said Eliza probably just wants to meet a celeb. That makes sense. Remember how she wanted to hear more about Benjamin when we were in New York?"

"That could be true," I say, "but I can tell that she's into Dylan and that she's jealous of you."

Paige shakes her head. "I don't think so, Erin."

"Then why would she use your phone like that, Paige? She could've just been open about it and asked you to invite Benjamin, you know, for the fun of it. Instead, she went behind your back and set it up."

"I don't know." Paige turns and smiles at me. "Maybe we're making too much of it, Erin. *C'est la vie.*"

"Okay." I nod. "This is your life. But don't say I didn't warn you."

Paige laughs. "Really, what's the worst that could happen? Benjamin shows up and we all have a few laughs about it. Who knows, maybe he and Eliza will hit it off."

"You wouldn't mind?"

She shrugs. "Not really."

I decide that Paige could be right. I probably am making too much out of it. Really, who cares if Eliza manipulated things to get Benjamin to hop a plane to France? Maybe it will make for an interesting show. So while Gabin drives with Paige reading the map for him, I watch for signs and eventually we find our way to Chateau Bertrand. A winding tree-lined driveway takes us up a hill where vineyards seem to stretch out for miles. We pass some stone buildings and finally pull up in front of what looks like a castle with high stone walls and rounded turrets. I think I understand why Eliza suffers from "princess syndrome."

"Wow," Paige gasps. "Is this the right place?"

"It is." Gabin nods as he parks the car, then stares at the building with a slightly surprised expression.

"Eliza's parents are quite wealthy," Dylan says.

"Ya think?" I climb out of the car and look at the amazing structure. It appears to be four stories high—maybe more since the turrets are above the fourth row of windows. "This place is amazing."

"Hey, it's about time," Eliza says as she comes out a tall front door. "Welcome to Chateau Bertrand." She heads straight for Dylan. "I just spoke to my mother and she's looking forward to meeting you tomorrow evening. She hopes you'll share some of your designs with her fashion show. I gave the coordinator Heather's cell phone number. I hope you don't mind."

"That's fine." He nods. "Nice digs you got here."

"Let me give you guys the full tour," Eliza offers as she links arms with him. "What took you so long to get here?"

"Didn't you get my message?" Paige asks as she picks up the pace to keep up with Eliza as she leads Dylan down a walkway.

Gabin and I hurry to catch up with them and, as I walk, I extract my camera from my bag, getting ready to get some shots.

"I got your message almost two hours ago," Eliza tells Paige. "I thought you'd be here before now. Did you get lost?"

"We were a little lost," Dylan admits. Paige is on his other side now and he links his other arm with her. Flanked by two beautiful blondes, Dylan looks like he's king for a day. "But it was a good kind of lost."

"Yes," Paige nods. "Bordeaux is such a beautiful part of the world. And this estate is absolutely magical, Eliza."

"A weekend in the country can be so refreshing." Eliza

seems to tighten her grip on Dylan and I wonder if there might be a tug-of-war before long.

We turn a corner coming around to the back of the house where a beautiful pool with fountains looks inviting.

"Hey, you made it," calls Taylor as she and JJ come over to greet us.

"Fran and the camera crew are already here," JJ informs us as he gets his camcorder ready to start filming. "They're getting situated in their rooms right now. The plan was to shoot some film after you guys arrived."

"Sounds good," Paige tells him.

JJ looks at Eliza. "I told Fran and the crew about your mother's request that the name and location of the chateau not be revealed on the show. And that's fine." He directs his camera at her. "Any accidental references will be cut."

"Thank you." Eliza pauses at a table near the pool where cold beverages are set up in elegant-looking pitchers and glasses. She invites us to help ourselves. "My parents don't mind sharing their home with guests, but they do appreciate their privacy."

"This place seems pretty private to me," I say as I look around. "Unless you're worried about helicopters."

Eliza looks up at the clear blue sky and laughs. "Well, I'm not expecting any paparazzi if that's what you mean."

"I be not so sure." Gabin gets a serious expression. "If paparazzi know there are two beautiful American TV stars, two fashion models, one famous American designer ... your privacy ... it might not be so much."

I almost add that there will be one more celebrity joining us—one who really could attract some unwanted media attention. But I will leave that to Paige to bring up.

Chapter
15

We're finishing up our drinks when Dylan thanks Eliza, once again, for inviting all of us up here. "I had no idea it was such a lovely place," he says with real admiration. "I'll be sure to convey my compliments to your mother." He waves his hands toward the seating area near the pool, complete with a huge stone fireplace and comfortable furnishings. It's really like a huge outdoor living room. "Such an attention to detail." He smiles. "As a designer, I can truly appreciate the beauty and style."

"And the crew and I appreciate your hospitality," JJ says as he directs his camera to Eliza. "Very generous."

"Speaking of hospitality ..." Paige begins slowly. "I hope you have plenty of room ... since you have another guest coming." Her eyes twinkle. "But, of course, you know that."

Eliza smiles but looks caught slightly off guard. "Who do you mean?"

I know JJ's camera is already running, but I also know this could get really good—or bad, depending on how it goes. I scramble to get my camcorder out too. As I power it up and remove the lens cover, there's this dead air space, kind of a pregnant pause, like Paige is in no hurry to answer Eliza. Fortunately, it can easily be cut. I suspect Paige is simply trying to give both JJ and me the chance to get this down on film. Finally I'm up and running and zoomed in on my sister.

Paige looks evenly at Eliza, her lips curved into a pleasant camera smile. "Well, Eliza, it seems that Benjamin Kross has accepted your generous invitation to join us here at the chateau. His flight arrives tomorrow morning. I assume you'll be in touch with him in regard to his travel arrangements from Bordeaux. I mean since he is *your* guest."

Eliza's neck flushes ever so slightly. "Oh, I hope you don't mind that I asked him," she says lightly to Paige. "I just thought it would be such fun to have him with the rest of us."

"Oh, I'm sure it will be fun," Paige says equally lightly.

Taylor chuckles as she sets her glass down. "This promises to be a very interesting weekend. I know I'm looking forward to meeting the notorious Benjamin Kross."

Paige clears her throat. "Ben has certainly made some stupid mistakes, but I wouldn't call him *notorious*."

Taylor smiles apologetically. "Sorry, Paige. I guess I take some getting used to. I have a tendency to speak without thinking sometimes."

"And Taylor is a tease," Dylan tells Paige.

"An outspoken tease," Taylor admits. "Especially when it comes to serious things like alcohol and addiction."

Eliza turns to Taylor with a worried expression. "Taylor Mitchell, please tell me you're *not* going to lecture the poor boy about rehab or AA or anything else. That would be so rude."

Taylor laughs. "I can't make any promises."

I try not to chuckle as I focus on Taylor. "Hey, I think that's a great idea," I tell her. "A little rehab probably wouldn't hurt old Benjamin a bit."

"Right …" Paige rests her forefinger alongside her chin. *"Rehab in the Vineyard.* That makes a lot of sense. Now if we could just come up with a fashion angle, we could include it in our show."

"It could be called *Stylish Rehab in the Vineyard,*" Taylor suggests. This is followed by a few more lame jokes and it becomes apparent that everyone is pretty much okay about Benjamin's surprise visit, which makes me think I probably did blow it out of proportion.

It's not long before Fran and the rest of the crew join us and, with cameras rolling, Eliza continues our tour of the property. Like a rich girl who's used to being a rich girl, she is rather nonchalant, bordering on bored, as she tells us about the several acres of botanical gardens as well as the two hundred acres of ancient grapevines. "Ours is considered a small winery," she explains as we continue on. "If any of you would like a tour of the vat rooms and wine cellars, our property manager, Henri, will arrange it."

"I'd enjoy that," Dylan says.

She turns and smiles so brightly at him that I'm surprised he doesn't reach for his sunglasses. "I'll speak to Henri for you." We pass by a long one-story stone building. Eliza explains that it's an old farmhouse with three large bedrooms — and where Fran and the film crew are staying. "It's not terribly fancy," she says. "But I think you'll be comfortable."

Next we return to the front part of what I'm calling "the castle" in my mind and since *chateau* is French for castle, I can't be too far off.

"The main house was built in the sixteenth century," Eliza continues. "Someone began restoring and updating it about ten years ago, and my mom's taken it from there. The work is mostly done now." She leads us through a grand entrance with polished stone floors and a massive stone staircase. "As you can see, my mom isn't trying to be historically accurate with the interior design." She motions toward a large open living area off to one side. It's surprisingly modern with a large leather sectional and contemporary chairs. Although the colors feel like they came straight from the vineyard — shades of olive green, gold, and burgundy.

Eliza leads us through a large dining room. This also has a contemporary feel with a long sleek wooden table and upholstered chairs, not to mention a killer view of the gardens. "My mother decided to go for comfort instead of history. Although some of the bedrooms have more of an old-world feel." She introduces us to Henri, explaining that he'll show us to our rooms. "Paige and Erin will be in the Françoise Room," she informs Henri, then turns to smile at us. "I hope you don't mind sharing."

"No, that's fine," Paige assures her.

"Gabin will be in the Laurant Room and Dylan will be in the Xavier Room." She continues rattling directions off as if she's quite comfortable playing hostess. Then, and not surprisingly, she offers to help Henri in showing the guests to their rooms. "And since the Laurant and Xavier rooms are near mine, I'll take the guys over to the east wing. Right this way, boys." The sound of victory rings in her footsteps as she leads the male guests up the stairs.

The guys are turning off their cameras now and Fran tells Paige and me that she'd like to have a short meeting with us and the crew before dinner. "Eliza said dinner's at seven thirty, so how about six at the farm house." With that settled, Henri shows us up two flights of stairs to our room on the third floor. "I will send someone up with your luggage later," he says a bit breathlessly. "May I get you anything else?"

Paige thanks him in French and closes the door. "I almost started to tip him," she whispers.

I chuckle. "Yeah, this feels kind of like a hotel."

"A five star hotel."

We pause to look at the delightfully round room, a result of the turret roof. Unlike the other parts of the house we saw, this room is furnished in a charming traditional French style.

"Now I feel like I'm really in a castle," I tell Paige as I peer out a window to see the courtyard below.

"Hopefully Eliza won't lock us up here and throw away the key," Paige teases as she heads for the bathroom. "Hey, it is nice in here," she calls out.

I move onto browsing the bookshelf next to the fireplace. It's fairly well stocked with a selection of novels, mysteries, and biographies that could keep me occupied for a couple of weeks. "As long as they served us food, I might not mind being imprisoned up here," I call to Paige.

I go over to the pair of full-sized beds, admiring the matching pale blue bedding, which feels like silk, and the blue velvet canopies with gold corded trim and tassels. I sit down on a bed and look around, taking in the gilt-framed oil paintings and other decorative touches. "This room feels very French," I tell Paige as she emerges from the bathroom.

"And the accoutrements in the bath aren't bad either." She holds up a wrist for me to smell. "Christian Dior."

"The perfect place for a pair of imprisoned princesses."

For the next hour or so, we both enjoy our "incarceration," but then it's time to go meet up with Fran and the crew. On the way across the grounds, we see Dylan and Gabin coming our way.

"Hey, we wondered if you girls were ever going to come back out," Dylan says as we stop to chat.

"We were just settling in," Paige tells him.

"And now we have a meeting for the show," I explain.

"Eliza gave us a private tour of the winery," Dylan says as the guys walk with us toward the farmhouse. "It was really interesting."

Gabin nods. "And *délicieux*."

"So you did a little tasting too?" Paige teases.

"How could we not?" Gabin asks.

"We'll see you later," I say as we reach the front door.

"At dinner," Paige calls.

We meet with Fran and the crew in the living room. And, although Eliza made it sound that this space wasn't much, I'm thinking it's pretty swanky for a "farmhouse." With overstuffed chairs, and charming antique accents, it would actually make a very nice home.

"Now I realize that this little jaunt to the country isn't our typical *On the Runway* episode, but I think if we keep the focus on the fact that it's two professional models, an American designer, and Gabin from Hermès, well, it's not a bad lineup. Right?" Fran asks.

Paige nods. "Absolutely. I think our fans will be very interested."

"So, don't worry too much about trying to stay fashion focused," Fran tells us. "Just be yourselves, hang with your friends, and forget the cameras are running."

Paige looks a little uneasy now.

"But what if things get sticky when Benjamin arrives tomorrow?" I ask.

"Let them get sticky." Fran smiles.

"But what if—"

"Erin," she says to me, "this is a reality show, is it not?"

"Yes, but ... for Paige's sake, it seems we should keep things from going nuts. I mean, fans expect Paige to be kind of in control. After all, it's not like we're turning into *Malibu Beach*, right?"

Fran seems to be considering this. "Even so, just relax and let whatever is going to happen, happen. We can always cut later. And you girls know how Helen Hudson feels. She has a certain vision for this show and she won't allow any scenes that take away from Paige's persona. We respect that Paige is what makes this show work."

"Okay then." I nod with uncertainty, reminding myself that it's not like I'm Paige's manager.

"It'll be fine," Paige assures me. "Not to mention interesting."

And so I figure, what am I worrying about? No one else seems the least bit concerned. For the rest of our meeting, we discuss logistics for catching some good film without taking all the fun out of the weekend. Mostly the plan is to have cameras around and ready to roll when needed.

"It's very gracious of Eliza to invite us," Fran says finally. "But we don't want to wear out our welcome."

I try not to roll my eyes at this. The fact is I'm not sure that we're as welcome as Fran assumes. I'm pretty sure the only reason we're here was to get Dylan here. But I could be wrong. I hope I'm wrong.

"Eliza invited everyone to the big house for dinner," Fran tells Paige and me as we're getting ready to leave. "She didn't mention whether this was a formal dinner though." She nods over the crew, who as usual are dressed very casually. "Do you know?"

Paige shrugs. "No one said anything about formal to me. It probably doesn't matter."

I look at Paige, who although not dressed "formally" looks more than presentable in the new Gucci dress that she picked up in Paris, and think it's easy for her to say it doesn't matter.

Fortunately, she's right. Dinner does turn out to be fairly casual, although Eliza, like Paige, looks like she put some effort into her appearance. She's also put some effort into the seating arrangement, flanking herself with Gabin and Dylan at one end of the long table and placing Paige and me on the other end with Taylor and the camera crew in between. Not that I care, but I can tell Paige is a bit miffed and I do find it interesting. Eliza seems quite pleased with herself, acting almost as if she thinks she's the queen of the castle and we're all here at her beck and command.

As expected, the wine flows freely during dinner. To my relief, Paige only has one glass of pinot noir, which she barely touches. However, everyone else, except for Taylor and me, seems to be enjoying the "fruit of the vine." After awhile, they start getting a little silly so I decide to excuse myself and set out to explore the house. I wind up in the billiards room and, since it looks like a pretty cool table and Eliza has said to make ourselves at home, I decide to try a few shots.

"Not bad," Taylor says as she enters the room in time to see me sinking two balls in the corner pocket.

"Thanks." I smile self consciously. "I'm actually not very good at this."

She laughs. "That sounds like an invitation to clean my clock."

"Hey, this is where the action is," JJ says as he and Gabin join us. "How about a game?"

Gabin looks a little unsure. "I am not expert in billiards."

I chuckle. "I'm not either."

"How about girls against the guys?" Taylor suggests. As it turns out, this makes for a more competitive match because Taylor and JJ are both pretty good. After best two out of three, Taylor and I win.

"When does Benjamin Kross get here?" Taylor asks me as we're putting the balls and pool cues away.

"I'm not really sure," I admit.

"Is Paige okay with it?" she questions.

JJ laughs and I shrug. "I guess she's okay. But it still seems weird that Eliza invited him. I mean especially *the way* she did it."

"By using Paige's phone?"

I nod. "It felt kind of underhanded to me."

Taylor makes a half smile. "Unfortunately that's just how some people work. And to be honest, I've been pretty deceitful myself in the past."

JJ looks skeptical. "You seem like a straightforward person to me."

She laughs. "That's because I'm trying to change my wicked ways. With God's help, that is. Trust me, I used to be a little devil. And I don't like to sound gossipy, but Paige should probably keep her eyes wide open this weekend."

"Hey, if anyone can hold her own, it's Paige Forrester," JJ

assures Taylor. "We've all seen that girl under fire before and she's usually pretty cool." He nods to me. "And when she's not, little sister steps in. Right, Erin?"

I sigh. "Hopefully that won't be necessary."

We hang around and visit for awhile longer, but finally JJ admits that he's exhausted from getting up extra early to get the van packed to come down here and that he's ready to call it a night. The rest of us follow suit and since the house is fairly quiet, we assume the others have turned in as well. Not that this is surprising since it's past midnight.

I'm surprised to discover that Paige isn't in our room yet. I consider calling her cell, although we've promised not to use our phones unnecessarily since it's pretty expensive, but when I try to turn on my iPhone, I realize the battery is dead—and I forgot to pack the charger cord. So I get ready for bed. I tell myself that I'll stay awake until Paige gets in, but before I know it I'm dozing off.

Chapter 16

When I wake up, the sun is shining in the window and Paige is in her bed. I tiptoe around the room, quietly getting dressed and ready to go out with my camera. I want to do some exploring around the estate and get some photos while the light is still good.

All seems quiet in the house and, feeling kind of like a thief, I make my way outside and into the gardens where the grass is still wet with dew. With all the blooming trees, green shrubbery, spring flowers, sculptures and fountains, it feels incredibly magical out here—and heavenly too. Like if I listen hard enough I might hear God whispering to me. I turn off my camera and sit down on a secluded bench. And with nothing else pressing in on me, I decide to spend some time alone with God. I thank him for all that he's done and is doing in my life, pray about the day ahead, and ask that he'll use me in some special way. Finally I just sit there quietly waiting, relaxing ... breathing ... and feeling that God is very near.

After awhile, I hear someone approaching and look up to

see what must be the gardener, clipping a hedge. I decide it's time to move on. But the moment remains with me, inside of me, and I think it will help get me through this day and the weekend. It's a good reminder of how important it is to take times like that—even when my schedule is hectic and busy. In fact, probably even more so then.

I continue around the estate, getting photos of whatever suits my fancy and just thoroughly enjoying myself, when suddenly I hear a male voice calling my name. When I turn to see who it is, I nearly fall over from shock to see Blake walking toward me. I blink and look again, thinking maybe I'm hallucinating, but, no, it's Blake.

"What are you doing here?" I demand as he runs up and hugs me.

"Didn't you get my message?"

"What message?"

"Oh, never mind," he says as he releases me from his embrace, then looks slightly dismayed. "Aren't you glad to see me?"

Now I'm not even sure how I feel, but I can tell I'm grinning. "I guess I actually am glad," I admit. "But surprised."

"So you really didn't know I was coming?" He frowns.

"No. I had no idea. Seriously, what's going on?"

"Well, I was with Ben the night that Paige invited him to come. We'd gone out for coffee to celebrate the settlement with Mia's family. Ben was so jazzed about coming here, and, out of the blue, he insisted that I should come with him—he even offered to pay my way."

"*Really?*" I shake my head, still trying to take this in.

"Yeah. At first I was kind of like, *no way, that's crazy* ... but Ben kept begging me to come, saying how I'd been such a help to him and that he needed someone to travel with . . . and I thought, *why not?*" Blake holds up his hands and grins. "And so here I am."

"This is just so weird," I say as I turn off my camera and slip it into my bag. "You and Benjamin are both here —"

"You're okay with that, aren't you?"

"Sure. Of course. Does Paige know Benjamin's here yet?"

"Yeah. She sent me out to find you. I guess breakfast is almost ready."

"Maybe we should go back then."

"Yeah. I'm starving." He puts his arm around my shoulders as we walk back. "Man, it's so great to see you, Erin. And your hair looks fantastic."

I reach up to touch my short hair. "Oh, yeah. I'd almost forgotten. Thanks." I smile at him. "And welcome to France."

"That was one long flight," he tells me as we walk. "I thought I'd want to hit the hay as soon as I got here, but now that I'm with you I feel totally energized. This is quite a place. Who knew you girls traveled in such style? I'm thinking maybe I should sign on with your show to carry your bags or give you pedicures or something."

I laugh. "Actually, this is Eliza's parents' place. I suspect the only reason we got invited here was so that Dylan Marceau would come."

"Huh?" Blake looks confused.

As we get closer to the house, I explain about how Dylan is kind of into Paige, but Eliza is kind of into Dylan.

"Oh?" His brow creases. "What about Paige?" he whispers. "Who's she into?"

I shrug. "You'd have to ask her."

The dining room is set up like a buffet this morning and

when we go in there, some of the guests are already starting to fill their plates.

"We'll be eating outside," Eliza explains to everyone. "Tables are set up by the pool." She looks directly at me with a puzzled expression.

"Have you met Blake yet?" I ask her.

She shakes her head. "I haven't had the pleasure."

I do a quick introduction, explaining his connection to Benjamin and the last-minute invite. "Hopefully there's room."

"Not as long as Benjamin doesn't mind sharing." She smiles as she shakes his hand. "Are you a reality TV star too?"

Blake looks slightly embarrassed. "No. I guess I'm just part of the Benjamin Kross entourage."

"And my good traveling buddy too," Benjamin adds as he comes into the room.

"There you are," Eliza says happily. "Did you get settled in okay?"

"Yeah." He smiles at her. "Thanks."

"Hopefully you won't mind sharing with Blake."

"Not at all. There's plenty of room."

Blake and I fill our plates then go out to the pool where several round tables are set up, each with four places as well as place cards. "Looks like we have assigned seating again," I tell Blake. This seems kind of weird to me, but I don't want to be rude.

"You're over here," Taylor calls out to me. I go over to where she and JJ are already starting their breakfast. "Who's the new guy?"

As I'm introducing Blake, Gabin comes out with his loaded plate and JJ calls him over to join us, pointing out his place card which is right next to mine—like we're a couple. "You sit here, buddy," JJ tells Gabin.

Eliza comes out and invites Blake to join her at her table. Blake gives Gabin and me a curious look then goes over to sit with Eliza. As I sit down it becomes clear to me that Eliza has arranged the seating. Paige and Ben are seated together. Meanwhile Dylan and Blake sit with Eliza, where she is acting like the Queen Bee again. It's hard not to laugh at how ridiculous this is—like does she honestly think that her arranged seating will somehow arrange people's affections?

Then I notice how Dylan's keeping what seems a wary eye on Paige and Ben. Paige, as usual, is being her normal charming self, happily chatting with Ben and Fran and Alistair as if there's no one on the planet more interesting. The gift of gab. As breakfast winds down, Dylan excuses himself and walks over to Paige's table, waiting as Paige introduces him to Benjamin.

"Do you still want to explore Bordeaux with me?" Dylan asks Paige.

"Absolutely." Paige nods and lays her napkin next to her plate.

"Are you coming too, Erin?" he calls over to me. "Eliza told us about some must-see places last night. And Gabin has offered to drive and serve as our guide as long as you come along."

"That's right." Gabin nods to me. "You will come, no?"

Okay, this is awkward at best. "But I—"

"I didn't have a chance to ask Erin about it yet," Paige says quickly. "And we didn't know Blake was coming with Ben so maybe—"

"It's okay," Blake says quickly. "You guys go ahead with

your plans. I know I kind of caught everyone off guard by crashing in on you like this."

"I'm sure we can find something around here to interest you," Eliza says pleasantly to Blake, but her expression is hard to read. "In fact, I'd be happy to give you and Benjamin the grand tour of the estate."

"That sounds like a good plan." Paige smiles at Benjamin. "After all, it *was* Eliza who invited you here. I'm sure she'll find something interesting for you boys to do."

I suspect, by Benjamin's expression, that he knows about Eliza swiping Paige's phone to set his visit up. Just the same, he doesn't look too happy about Paige's nonchalant attitude.

"Ben and I probably won't last long anyway," Blake says. "It feels like it's been a week since I've seen a real bed."

"You came to the right place," Eliza says in a flirty tone.

And just like that, it seems settled. I'm going to Bordeaux with Gabin, Dylan, and Paige. Everyone else appears to be staying here. I tell Blake I'll see him later, then after Paige and I go to our room to get some things, I mention my suspicions—that I think Eliza is up to something.

"I'm sure she is," Paige says as she touches up her makeup.

"And you're okay with that?"

She shrugs as she reaches for her Kelly bag. "Not much I can do about it."

"Ben looked kind of put out."

"I explained to him that it was Eliza who invited him. He seemed to understand."

"Well, I still feel a little guilty for leaving Blake behind," I admit as we're heading back downstairs.

"Don't worry, they'll be fine."

I tell myself that Paige is probably right as we go outside

and see Gabin and Dylan waiting for us by the car. JJ and Taylor pull up in the camera crew van and announce that they plan to tag along. "Fran thought I might get some good footage today," JJ explains.

"And I'm going to be his helper," Taylor says.

He laughs. "The only help I want from you is to be on the other side of my camera."

Bordeaux turns out to be an interesting place and Gabin is the perfect guide. Although I'm sure Paige would prefer more shopping, I'm grateful that Gabin insists on taking us to several museums. Then we eat a divine lunch at a very cool bistro. The day slips by quickly and suddenly we're scrambling to make it back to the chateau in time for dinner.

Paige calls Eliza to explain that we're running a few minutes late and that Taylor and JJ should be there ahead of us. As Gabin speeds down the winding country road, Paige announces that tonight's dinner is going to be "formal." She drops her phone into her bag. "That means we need to hurry and get changed as soon as we get there," she quietly tells me. "Eliza sounded a bit impatient."

Gabin makes fairly good time and it's about 7:45 when we reach the chateau. Paige and I do hurry and, as a result, I know I look slightly thrown together as we head back down. But Paige, as always, is sweet perfection as we join the others where hors-d'oeuvres are being served in the living room. Everyone looks very nice—very grown up, and JJ, still in his street clothes, is there with his camera running.

"Eliza invited me to film part of tonight's dinner," he quietly tells Paige and me. "Fran and the others are fixing dinner for themselves in the farmhouse. I'll join them in awhile."

I wonder if he feels like hired help now, and if it's a letdown after having been previously included. I also wonder if Eliza purposely uninvited Fran and the crew and, if so, why?

The dinner party is moving now as Eliza leads us into the dining room, where crystal and silver are shimmering in the candlelight. With fresh flowers and white linen, the table looks as if Eliza is expecting royalty. And, sure, it's impressive, but I suddenly wish I was with Fran and the crew in the farmhouse.

Not surprisingly, Eliza has arranged the seating again. I'm slightly surprised that she didn't seat herself with Dylan this time. I'm wondering if she's taken a shine to Benjamin or even Blake since both of them are seated on either side of Queen Eliza. Not that I care particularly. It's just interesting. I find my place card between Gabin and Dylan, and Gabin, ever the gentleman, pulls out my chair for me to sit. Soon we are all seated and I think we look like a scene from an old movie. Eight for dinner at eight.

"Did you have a good time in Bordeaux?" Benjamin's gaze is locked onto Paige. I can see longing in his eyes and I know he's not happy with the Dylan situation.

"It's a delightful town," Paige tells him.

"You should check it out before you go home," I say as our soup is served.

"When *do* you go home?" Paige asks.

Benjamin's brow creases. "Are you trying to get rid of me already?"

"No, of course not." Paige laughs lightly. "I was just curious."

As Benjamin reaches for a bottle of red wine, generously filling his glass, I notice Taylor's brows lift. "So ... Benjamin," she says slowly. "I read about your car accident awhile back.

It sounded like a nightmare. I'm curious about how it's all shaking down."

"It's pretty much history now," he tells her. "My attorney got the Renwicks to settle out of court and I'm scheduled to do a special episode on *Malibu Beach* that should put the rumors to rest."

"Rumors?" Taylor questions him.

"You know how the media can be. The sooner the press forgets about this whole thing, the happier everyone will be." Benjamin flashes his famous Hollywood smile at her, then lifts his wine glass as if to make a toast. "In fact that's the main reason I decided to come over here — *to celebrate.*"

"So you're celebrating *not* going to trial?" Taylor asks him.

"Partially." Benjamin's glass clinks against his plate as he sets it down. "But more than that I'm celebrating getting my life back, as well as my movie deal."

"Benjamin was telling me about that today," Eliza says quickly. "It sounds like it's going to be a hit."

"I notice you're drinking," Taylor says to him.

"*Taylor,*" Eliza warns. "Benjamin is my guest."

Ben gives Taylor an easy smile. "Hey, this is a winery. You know what they say ... *when in Rome.*"

Taylor picks up her glass of water. "Not for everyone."

I decide to show my solidarity with Taylor by holding up my water glass too. "Cheers!"

Blake chuckles as he holds up his water too. "Here's to sobriety."

Eliza sighs loudly. "Thanks a lot, Taylor. It was so nice of you to divide the table like this. *Bon appetit,* everyone."

"Hey, you can't blame me for being honest," Taylor protests. "I'm a girl who likes to speak her mind."

"So what is it you're trying to say?" Benjamin challenges her.

She looks evenly at him. "Just that you might want to rethink some things."

"What sort of things?" I can tell by his tone and his smile that he's hoping to charm her. But I can tell by her expression that it's hopeless.

"Well, from what I've heard and read about the accident, as well as some articles related to your TV career and personal life, I'd say you have a serious drinking problem, Benjamin."

"Oh, Taylor." He chuckles. "Please, tell me you're not the kind of person who believes what the tabloids say. I'll bet they've said some sensational things about you that aren't true. You know how they treat celebs."

She laughs. "Actually, I don't think the tabloids are terribly interested in me."

"Not yet anyway." Dylan winks at her. "But it won't be long."

"And if that ever is the case," she continues, "I hope to be an open book. I've never made a secret of the fact that I needed rehab treatment for my own alcohol addiction — or that I still attend AA meetings. I'll tell anyone who wants to know."

"That's a fact," Eliza confirms. "And, take it from me, it can be pretty embarrassing too."

Benjamin looks at Taylor with surprise. "*You* were in rehab?"

Taylor nods. "Yep. A good friend confronted me after a particularly bad binge in Las Vegas. I will always be thankful for her intervention."

With a slightly thoughtful expression, Benjamin nods. "My congratulations to you, Taylor. But just because you needed rehab doesn't necessarily mean that I or anyone else does."

"But it doesn't mean that you don't either." She smiles graciously at him. "It's nice to see you're not offended by me bringing it up."

He lifts his wine glass. "Not at all. Everyone is entitled to their own opinions." He takes a sip, pausing to savor it. "Excellent vintage, Eliza. My compliments to the wine master."

Eliza starts talking about one of their elite wines. "It's an amazing Marguax that was bottled the year after my parents bought the chateau," she explains, "and it's already gaining some great international attention."

"Do you mind saying what a bottle like that would go for?" Benjamin asks her. "I'm just curious."

She gives him a sly smile, then whispers something in his ear, and his eyes get wide. *"Seriously?"*

She nods and chuckles.

"Okay, share with the group," Dylan tells her. "How much?"

"Just under a thousand a bottle right now, but it'll go up each year."

"No way!" I stare at her. "How can one bottle of wine possibly be worth a thousand bucks?"

She makes a catty smile. "If you were a connoisseur you would know, Erin. As it is you don't even *drink* wine. How could you possibly understand?"

"Maybe if I was crazy I would understand," I shoot back at her.

"Did we taste any of that on our tour?" Benjamin asks.

She laughs then shakes her head. "No, that's not usually available for sampling ... that is, unless you're a very serious shopper."

"Maybe I am," he tells her. "It might be fun to bring something like that home for my parents."

"You'd buy a case?" she asks.

He looks uncertain. "Well, maybe not a whole case."

"A case would be twelve thousand dollars," I proclaim.

"Oh, you little math whiz," Eliza teases.

"I'm just saying that's a lot of money." I lean back as an entrée is set before me. "Do you realize you could care for four thousand African orphans for a whole month with that much money—and I'm talking food, clothes, medicine, and school."

"Wow, you really are a math whiz," Taylor tells me.

"Again with the African orphans," Eliza says in a bored way.

"Sorry," I tell her as I see my sister giving me a warning look. "I suppose that's not very polite dinner conversation."

"I don't know," Taylor says as her entrée is set down. "I think people like us—you know, the ones who can afford it—we *need* to talk about those kinds of things."

"Maybe so," I agree. "But not at dinner. Not as a guest anyway." However, as I pause to remember which fork to pick up, I'm thinking … *after dinner* I can talk about it. And if anyone will listen to me, maybe I will.

Chapter

17

After we finish dessert, Eliza quietly speaks to Henri about something, and he nods then leaves. "I have an idea," she tells everyone. "I'll take you down to Daddy's private wine cellar for our *fromages*."

"That sounds delightful," Dylan says.

"And perhaps we'll do some tasting as well," Eliza says with a twinkle in her eye.

"In that case, I'll pass," Taylor announces.

"I will too," I say, and then Blake chimes in.

Eliza frowns at us. "I can understand why Taylor wants to pass, but Erin and Blake too? Why would you pass up an opportunity to taste a real *Bordeaux Marguax*?"

"Come on," Paige urges me. "Eliza is right. You should at least sample it."

I roll my eyes and just shake my head.

"Do try it, Erin," Gabin says. "This is your opportunity to expérience France. Is *échantillon*."

"Taste it for Mom," Paige tells me. "She'll get a kick knowing we tried such an expensive wine."

I consider this.

"Is it because you're a Christian?" Eliza presses me.

I shrug. "That's not really it. Mostly it's because I don't like the taste."

"Have you *tasted* Bordeaux Marguax before?" Dylan asks me.

"I really don't see what the big deal is," I protest. "Why all this pressure?"

"You know ..." Eliza directs this to both me and Blake. "I've heard that Jesus turned water into wine. According to my mom it was his first miracle."

"So?" I look at her.

"So, maybe there was a reason for it," she tells me.

"Come on, Erin," Paige tugs on my arm. "Just have a tiny little taste."

"Fine." I hold up my hands. "If it means that much to you, I'll try it. It's not like it's a sin to drink wine."

"It is for me," Taylor admits. "Don't get me wrong, I'm not saying that it's wrong for everyone." She looks at Benjamin. "But it is for *some people*."

"Okay," Blake says. "If Erin tries it, I will too."

"I don't want to be a bad influence," I tell him.

He laughs. "I'm a big boy, Erin. I can make up my own mind. Besides, the drinking age here makes it perfectly legal anyway."

We trek down the narrow stone steps and into a spacious cool room with low ceilings. Candlelight illuminates the bottle-filled wooden shelves along the walls. Comfortable leather chairs are arranged around a large wooden table, which is already set up with a large cheese and fruit platter and an opened bottle of wine and sparkling glasses.

After we sit down, Eliza pours a small bit of red wine into each glass. She shows us how to properly sample the wine by swirling it around in the glass, looking at it, smelling it. But when I smell it I'm still not sure I want to drink any. I'm worried that I'm being pressured into something against my will. As the others are sampling, I set my glass down.

"You're not going to even try it?" Eliza demands.

I shrug. "Does it really matter?"

Her expression tells me that maybe it does matter. "Let's make a deal," she says suddenly.

"What?"

"If you sample the wine, I'll contribute to those African orphans you keep talking about."

"Really?"

She lets out an exasperated sigh, then nods. "Yes. I'll contribute the value of one bottle of wine. How's that?"

"Do you know that one bottle of wine would take care of one child for nearly three years?"

She seems surprised by this.

"Okay, it's a deal." I lift my glass. "Here's to the child you'll be helping." I take a cautious sip and, really, it's not that bad.

"So?" she asks hopefully.

"It's fine," I tell her. "I'm just not that into it, okay?"

"Maybe you should try another sip," Dylan suggests. "More slowly this time."

I look at him. "Are you willing to contribute to the orphan fund too?"

He laughs then nods. "Sure, why not?"

So, again, I hold up my glass, make a toast, and take a sip. I'm still unimpressed.

"So?" Eliza asks again. "Any better this time?"

"I'm sure it's a great wine," I say as I study the red liquid remaining in my glass. "It's just not my cup of tea."

"And if you stop drinking it," Taylor says suddenly, "I will match Eliza's contribution to the orphan fund."

I set my glass down and nod. "It's a deal."

"Why don't we all contribute," Paige says suddenly. And, to my surprise, everyone agrees and I offer to handle the donations.

"Anyone want to play some pool?" Taylor asks as she stands. "I'm getting claustrophobia down here."

"Sure," I agree. Gabin and Blake both say they'd like to shoot some pool as well, so our group splits up as we head for the billiards room. To my relief, Taylor asks to team up with Gabin, which allows me to partner with Blake. But I can still feel a little tension in the air and I hope that Gabin hasn't assumed that I'm more interested in him that I am.

We're just starting our third game when we hear raised voices nearby. "It sounds like Eliza's ready to tear into someone," Taylor says as she sets her cue down. We all go out into the living room area where Paige and Eliza appear to be facing off.

"I don't think you understand," Paige is calmly telling Eliza. "I was only saying that—"

"I know what you were saying," Eliza shouts back at her. "You were calling me a slut and—"

"I was not." Paige firmly shakes her head. "I was simply saying that you seem to need a guy by your side, not that you were a—"

"And you're saying that you don't enjoy having a guy around?" Eliza demands.

"I enjoy it," Paige says, "but I can live without it too."

"That's true enough," Ben says with irritation. "You have no problem pushing me away anytime you like."

"What is that supposed to mean?" Paige asks him.

"You know what it means."

Dylan steps up next to Paige. "I think that's a very mature quality. I appreciate a woman who isn't overly needy."

"Oh, you mean *like me*?" Eliza shoots at him. "Am I overly needy?"

"I never said that," Dylan says calmly.

"You don't *have* to say it." With her hands on her hips, Eliza glares at him with a reddened face.

"I think we should all call it a night," Paige says as she makes her way toward the door. "I'm sorry if I offended you, Eliza. It's not what I meant to—"

"Oh, sure." Eliza steps in front of Paige. "Just stir things up and then run away and hide. Act as if you're the victim. *Right?*"

Paige looks evenly at Eliza. "I never said I was the victim. But I am tired and I think it's time to—"

"This is *my* house!" Eliza shouts at her. "And you are my guest. And I say when it's time to—"

"Eliza," Dylan says firmly. "I think Paige is right. It is getting late. Please, excuse us." He cuts in front of Eliza, takes Paige by the arm, and appears as if he plans to escort her away.

"You better not take her to your room!" Eliza shouts after them.

"Eliza," Taylor says as she steps in. "You seriously need to chill."

"*Shut up!*" Eliza snaps at her. "This is my house and you don't tell me what to do!"

"Eliza's right," Benjamin says. "Dylan better not be taking Paige to his room." Suddenly he's taking off after them.

I nudge Blake and he hurries to catch up with Ben, saying, "Hey, buddy, slow down."

"What are *you* staring at?" Eliza demands as she looks at me.

"Nothing," I say quietly.

Eliza lets loose with some choice words and stomps away.

"Wow," I say to Taylor and Gabin. "I wonder what made her so mad."

Taylor sighs. "Same old, same old."

"What?"

"Eliza wants what Eliza wants—and she can't stand it when she doesn't get it. And drinking seems to exacerbate the problem." Taylor shakes her head. "I think I'll go check on her."

Now it's just Gabin and me, standing in the foyer. "I think I better check on Paige," I finally say.

"Yes." He nods. "But ... uh, I first ... I have a question?"

"What?"

"Is Blake ... is he ... uh ... your ... uh ..."

"You mean is he my boyfriend?" I say for him.

"*Oui*. Yes. Is he?"

I frown. "Not exactly. But he's a *very good* friend." I smile at Gabin. "And you are a very good *friend* too."

He nods with what seems a sad expression. "I see."

"*Bonsoir*, Gabin." I smile at him.

To my surprise, he gently takes my hand and kisses it. "*Bonsoir*, Erin."

I'm sure I look slightly shocked as I tell him goodnight again then hurry up the stairs to the third floor, where I find Paige getting ready for bed.

"Are you okay?" I ask her.

"Sure, I'm fine." She turns and really looks at me. "How about you?"

I tell her about my little exchange with Gabin.

She shakes her head. "Poor Gabin. I think he was smitten with you."

"Smitten?" I frown as I kick off my shoes. "I don't think so, Paige. For starters, I told him from the beginning I wasn't interested in a serious relationship."

"So you make the rules for the heart?"

"I tried to lay my cards on the table for him," I protest.

"But surely you could see that he was really into you, couldn't you?"

I press my lips together and consider this. "I don't know," I say slowly. "Honestly, this whole thing has caught me off guard. You're the one who's used to dealing with guys. I'm the novice. I don't know what I should've done differently. I thought maybe he was just being overtly attentive because he's French."

She laughs. "Fine. If you say so."

Okay, now I do feel guilty. Should I have seen this coming? Should I have done something to prevent it? I never in a million years meant to hurt Gabin. Wouldn't continuing a relationship with him seem like it would do just that?

"Chateau Bertrand is a beautiful place," I say sadly as I unzip my dress, "but I'll be glad to get out of here."

"Did the fireworks show fizzle after Dylan and I made our exit?" she asks as she rubs some lotion into her elbows.

"Pretty much."

"I was worried that Eliza's mom was going to walk in and we'd be in the middle of it. Eliza said she was due to come home tonight."

"That's right, it's the local fashion show tomorrow."

"Which is why we both need a good night's rest." Paige turns off the light by her bed. "I have a feeling tomorrow is going to be rough."

I'm actually wondering if we'll even be allowed to do the fashion show tomorrow. The way Eliza was acting tonight, I wouldn't be surprised if she threw Paige and me and our crew out the door before breakfast. And, the truth is, I would be relieved. Too much stress.

But tomorrow comes and Eliza acts as if nothing whatsoever happened last night. Oh, she's a little more subdued than usual and I can't help noticing her "arranged seating" has fallen by the wayside. For the most part, she is being fairly nice. When her mother waltzes into breakfast, Eliza politely introduces her to everyone and I begin to think last night's drama was just a crazy dream and that today will be smooth sailing after all.

But I quickly see that's not going to happen and so, as soon as I finish breakfast, I slip away to spend some time alone. More than ever I feel like I'm in over my head. I still feel uneasy about Gabin, and whether or not I've hurt him and if there is something I should do. I bow my head and ask for God to lead me, to give me some direction, and to help me to live my life in a way that honors him. I ask him to bless this day . . . hopefully without any more fireworks. Then, as I'm walking back to the house, I see Gabin putting his suitcase in the trunk of his rental car.

"What are you doing?" I ask him.

He comes over to me with a serious expression. "My apology," he says. "It is time for me to go."

"You don't want to stay for the fashion show?" I ask.

"No, I must go."

I reach out and take his hand. "Thank you for being my good friend," I tell him. "I hope you're not sorry you came."

He smiles as he squeezes my hand. "No ... not sorry. It is my pleasure to know you, Erin."

"And mine too." My hand slips out of his and I stand there wishing there was something—anything—I could say to make this easier. "Thank you for being my friend," I tell him.

"*Au revoir, mon cheri.*"

"*Au revoir.*" I feel unexpectedly sad as I watch him drive away. I wonder if maybe I liked him more than I realized. And yet, I know that's silly. He and I are so different, different worlds. I'm sure it's simply the romance of this place messing with my mind.

"Where's Gabin going?" Blake asks me as he joins me in the front of the house.

"Home." I turn to him with a forced smile.

"Oh?"

"It was time." I start walking back toward the house.

"Are you sad that he left?" Blake's voice is laced with concern.

"No, not really. I just hope I didn't hurt him."

"You mean because he was into you?"

"I don't know."

Blake opens the door, stepping aside to let me pass. "He was, you know."

Wanting to defuse this moment, or just avoid it, I playfully punch him in the arm. "And did that make you jealous?" I say in a teasing tone.

He makes a sheepish smile. "Maybe."

Thankfully, the fashion show is fairly small and doesn't take too long. Because it's a fundraiser, there seems to be more focus on the food and wine and socializing than on actual fashion. I can tell that both Paige and Fran are a little disappointed. As we ride back to the house, I remind them that this weekend was for an episode that we hadn't even planned on initially.

"So even if we don't use it, it's no big deal, right?" I say lightly.

"I suppose." Paige sighs. "But it's sure been a lot of effort for nothing."

Fran laughs. "Hey, we got some good footage as well as a nice little vacation on a lovely estate."

"Some of us had more of a vacation than others," Paige says. I tell Fran a bit about Eliza's little fireworks show last night.

"Too bad the camera guys didn't catch that," Fran says.

"Who knows with that girl?" Paige tells her. "That might not be the last of it."

And when we're back at the house, I wonder if Paige might be right about Eliza. Despite her invitation to everyone, including the camera crew, to enjoy a late lunch by the pool, she is acting very chilly toward Paige and me, and I get the feeling that the sooner Eliza sees the last of us, the better it will be for everyone. I wish we could just pack it up and go right now, but our return tickets to Paris are for tomorrow.

After an hour or so of basking in the Bordeaux sunshine (and the Eliza frost) Paige and I decide to retreat to our tower room and lay low until dinner time. If I had my way, I'd grab a ride back to Paris tonight. Instead, I decide to pray about the evening, asking God to bring something good out of what feels like a waste of time—and at the very least avoid any bloodshed.

Chapter 18

Thankfully, tonight's dinner, our last meal in the *chateau*, is not a formal affair. I'm also relieved to see that Fran and the crew have been invited, which seems to work as a buffer of sorts. Because the spring evening is unusually balmy, we are eating outside. Mrs. Wilton makes an appearance, but she doesn't seem comfortable with what she calls "Eliza's friends" and she doesn't stick around for long.

After her mother excuses herself, Eliza starts opening more bottles of wine. And, although we're done with our meal, she continues to encourage everyone to sample more wines and to "drink up," like she wants everyone to get loopy. Unfortunately, Benjamin seems more than willing to comply.

"Haven't you had enough?" Taylor asks him as he generously refills his glass.

"Am I about to get your rehab spiel again?" he snipes back.

"Only if you need it," she says sweetly. "And I think you probably do."

He leans closer to her and smiles. "You are seriously pretty, Taylor Mitchell. I wish I'd known you back *before* you jumped on the wagon because I'm sure that you and I would've been *really* good friends back then."

"Kind of like Mia Renwick?" She sighs and shakes her head.

Benjamin looks like someone punched him as he turns away.

"Oh, Taylor," Eliza growls at her. "Give it a rest, okay?"

"You mean I should pretend that it's okay for Ben to get drunk here tonight, when we all know that a young woman was killed because of—"

"Lighten up!" Eliza snaps back at her. "You are a serious buzzkill."

Paige tries to gently intervene, but that only makes Eliza madder. It's obvious that this can only get worse—like battle lines have been drawn and the big artillery is about to come out. I'm getting ready to excuse myself and make a fast exit.

"Hey, everyone," Blake says loudly. "I have a fun idea."

"What?" Eliza turns to him with a bottle of wine still in her hand.

"Something we can all enjoy," he says with a charming smile.

"And that is?" Eliza shows the tiniest spark of interest.

"Well, I discovered a pretty cool place over near the vineyard," he tells her. "A big fire pit with benches all around it. Like someone has had bonfires there before."

"Oh, yeah." She nods. "The fire pit my dad and brother built."

"So how about if we go make a fire and hang there?" Blake removes the bottle of wine from Eliza's hand, placing it on the table. "I was only a boy scout for a couple of years, but I'm sure I can still make a fire."

"That's an awesome idea," Dylan says with enthusiasm. "I haven't been to a bonfire since I was a kid."

Suddenly everyone is on board and we all take off in different directions. Some of us go up to change shoes and grab sweaters. Others head for the fire pit to get it started. Before long, Paige and I are equipped with flashlights and trekking through the darkness with several others. By the time we get there, a fire is crackling and JJ is warming up his harmonic awhile Alistair tunes a guitar. "This was hanging on the wall in the farmhouse," he tells us. "We'll find out if it's more than just a decoration."

"I feel like I'm at sleepover camp," Paige says happily as we sit down on a log bench.

"Me too," I say. "Too bad we don't have the ingredients for s'mores."

It feels like whatever animosity was churning back at the chateau is slowly fading away. And it's not long until JJ and Alistair start sounding pretty good in the music department. And just like that we're all sitting there around the fire and singing along to whatever camp and folk songs we can come up with and actually remember the words to — it's actually a lot of fun.

But after awhile we get kind of stuck. No one can think of a new song and all we hear is the snapping of the logs. Then Dylan stands up and clears his throat. "Okay, kids, do I have a treat for you." He chuckles. "It's a poem I memorized in the sixth grade." In a dramatic and mysterious voice he begins to recite it.

"There are strange things done in the midnight sun
By the men who moil for gold;
The Arctic trails have their secret tales

That would make your blood run cold;
The Northern Lights have seen queer sights,
But the queerest they ever did see
Was that night on the marge of Lake Lebarge
I cremated Sam McGee.

He pauses, waiting for our reaction of dramatic gasps, and then he continues in his creepy low voice.

Now Sam McGee was from Tennessee,
where the cotton blooms and blows.
Why he left his home in the South to roam
'round the Pole, God only knows.
He was always cold, but the land of gold
seemed to hold him like a spell;
Though he'd often say in his homely way
that he'd "sooner live in hell."

We all sit spellbound as Dylan recites this long, gory poem about how one gold miner cremates his frozen friend. We clap wildly when he finally finishes.

"That was brilliant, man." JJ gives him a high five.

Paige shakes her head in disbelief. "Who knew Dylan Marceau, the brilliant designer, also recites poetry?"

"Anyone else with hidden talents?" JJ asks.

Eliza stands up and grabs Taylor's hand to join her. "Let's sing *Bloody Mary* from South Pacific." So the two of them, with really good voices, suddenly break into the rousing song, complete with an interesting dance routine. Once again, we all clap and cheer as they take their bows.

"Who's next in our *Bordeaux Has Talent* lineup?" Fran calls out.

Blake grabs my hand, pulling me to my feet. "What are you doing?" I ask frantically. "I have no talent, remember?"

He whispers in my ear that we are about to sing *Amazing Grace* to the tune of *Gilligan's Island* like we sometimes do in fellowship group. And although I'm reluctant, I agree. To my relief, Taylor actually stands up and joins us which greatly improves the musical quality of our contribution. Again, once we're done, everyone claps. But it might be from relief.

"That song actually means a lot to me," Blake says as Taylor and I both sit down. "And if it's okay, I'd like to tell you why." Since no one protests, Blake continues, sharing his testimony about how he grew up in a Christian home, but how he finally had to come to his faith on his own. "God doesn't have grandchildren," he says earnestly. "I finally realized that just because my parents were Christians didn't mean that I was. I had to take my own spiritual journey toward God. And it's been really good. I'm the first one to admit I'm not perfect, not even close, but God is changing me, making me into a new person, a person I am learning to like. I know we're all at different places in life," he says finally, "but I just wanted to let you guys know that God loves each of us—and he wants us to love him too. I want to challenge everyone here to think about that—to give God a chance." Blake shrugs like he's kind of embarrassed. "I guess that's all."

Again we all clap—some with more enthusiasm than others. Then Taylor gets up and tells a different but similar story. She talks about how she was lost and miserable and how she used alcohol as an escape. "I know Ben's sick of hearing me talk about rehab, but here's the truth: *I never would've made it through rehab and sobriety without God's help*. That's what made all the difference. And even though Eliza wants to strangle me sometimes, she can attest to the truth." She points at Eliza. "I *have* changed, haven't I? And that's because of God. *Right?*"

Eliza nods. "Yeah. Taylor used to be the wildest girl I knew."

"But now you're going for that award?" Benjamin teases her. Eliza just looks down at the fire, shaking her head as if she doesn't want that prize.

"This has been a cool evening," JJ says as he gets his harmonica out of his pocket. "It brings a certain song to mind. Feel free to sing along." He starts to play and after the first stanza there are some hoots of laughter along with some groans.

Fran slaps her knee and lets out a big chortle. "I just knew we'd sing *Kumbaya* before this was over and done!" But she joins in the singing and I even get a feeling that she's enjoying it as much as I am. And as crazy-corny as this whole campfire thing seemed at first, I can tell that everyone has kind of enjoyed it. Maybe sometimes we just need to act like kids around the campfire again. It sure beats drinking and fighting.

As we trek back to the chateau, I grab Blake's hand and commend him for coming up with the bonfire idea. "I think it was inspired," I tell him.

He chuckles. "Yeah, it seemed pretty out there at first, but then I thought maybe it was God."

"Absolutely." I nod. "Definitely God."

Chapter

19

Paige, Dylan, and I ride the train back to- gether to Paris on Tuesday morning. Meanwhile Blake and Benjamin are on their own—sort of. Eliza told them they were welcome to stay on at the chateau. Although Blake really wants to come to Paris and I suspect Benjamin does too, Paige wasn't giving him much encouragement.

Anyway, I'm not sure if the three of us are simply tired or talked out, but it's pretty quiet in the first class car. Finally, I wonder if it's me. Maybe Dylan would like to talk to Paige alone—in fact, I'm fairly certain he does. I head off in search of coffee and pastry and don't go back until we're coming into Paris. At the terminal, Dylan hugs both Paige and me, but I can tell that her hug is more intense. Then we part ways with him. His plan is to grab a cab back to his hotel where he will pack up and head back to New York later in the day.

Fran picks us up in the town car, going over this after-noon's itinerary. "We have time to stop at the hotel for about an hour," she explains, "to drop things off and do hair and makeup before the next interview." She smiles at Paige. "And, don't forget, this is our *pièce de résistance*."

"Who is it?" I ask absently.

"Givenchy!" they both exclaim.

"Oh." I nod as if this means something more to me.

At the hotel, Paige carefully selects an ensemble that she is confident will please the Givenchy people. She even makes me dress a bit nicer than my usual Camera Girl outfit, although I keep it simple with a black skirt, white blouse, and a black cashmere cardigan. Next to Paige, who is wearing a pink and gray plaid jacket and pink skirt, I'm sure I look downright boring.

"This could be our best interview of the whole trip," she tells me as Luis finishes up with her hair.

"Next," he calls to me.

"But I don't need—"

"Erin!" Paige points to the chair. "Sit."

I cooperate and listen as Paige drones on about how Givenchy was ahead of his time, how his designs revolutionized fashion, how he is one of her all-time favorites. "You know Hubert Givenchy designed for both Audrey Hepburn and Grace Kelly," she says as we head outside of the hotel.

"Not to mention Jackie O," Fran adds as we get into the car.

"If we're lucky, we'll get a word with Riccardo Tisci," she tells me as we're riding through the city.

"Not Givenchy himself?" I ask.

She laughs. "That is doubtful since Hubert's quite ancient and not really part of the company now."

"If he's even still alive," Fran adds.

"So who is Riccardo Tisci?" I ask Paige.

"The main Givenchy designer, and very talented," she explains.

As we enter the building, I'm expecting this to be a pretty interesting interview, but I begin to notice a pattern as we're being given the usual tour. It seems that the models I'm seeing, both in photos and in the fitting room, are all extremely thin. That concerns me. Not that I will mention it here, but it's a reminder that I've been promised our show will do an episode dedicated to the health issues and concerns that are part of this industry. I am determined to make sure that we follow through with it.

For now I will remain safely and quietly behind my camera, focusing on Paige as she does the final wrap-up of the interview. For some reason she seems frustrated. I suspect it's because on the last leg of our tour, we've been assisted by a young designer named André. For some reason André has been a bit on the cool and aloof side. In fact, it reminds me a bit of the day we did *Vogue Paris* last week. No matter how hard Paige tries, or how friendly she is, it's like André is keeping her at arm's length.

"Thank you for your time," she tells him, still smiling brightly. "Givenchy is definitely one of the most important leaders in Parisian fashion — in fact the fashion world at large. And we are honored to have spent this time with you."

He nods with a slightly bored expression. "But before you go, I must ask you one question."

Paige brightens. "Certainly. Anything."

He nods over to me. "And who is this?"

"Oh, I'm sorry," Paige tells him. "I forgot you weren't with us when we did introductions. This is my younger sister, Erin. She's part of the show."

To be polite I let my camera down and give him a slightly chilly smile. To my surprise he moves in closer, as if he's examining me like a bug under a magnifying glass. I actually step back. He laughs. "You do not realize why I am looking at you?"

I shake my head no.

"You are so much like Audrey Hepburn that you caught my eye."

"Oh." I nod. "Thank you."

"I wish Hubert Givenchy could see you."

"We'll be happy to send you a DVD of our show," Paige tells him. I can hear a trace of irritation in her voice. "Perhaps you can share that with him."

André reaches for my chin, tilting it slightly to the left. "Ah ... yes. You would be good in print."

"Thank you very much," Paige says in a formal tone. "I'm sure Erin will keep that in mind."

He lets go of my chin, looking me up and down carefully, like he's taking some kind of inventory. "Of course, you would never do on the runway."

"No," I say quietly. "I'm aware of that."

He smiles. "But if you are ever interested in print modeling—"

"Thank you," I say quickly. "But I'm not interested in any kind of modeling. I prefer being on this side of the camera." I put my camera in front of my face again and continue to film.

"Too bad," he says abruptly. He turns and without even saying good-bye, leaves the room.

"And so here we are," Paige says to the still-running cameras. "Givenchy Paris where my little sister has just turned to print modeling." She laughs, but I can tell she doesn't think it's funny. "And remember, you never know who's watching ... so don't forget to always put your best foot forward." She pauses to hold out a sleek black pump. "And that would be Christian Louboutin today. This is Paige Forrester for *On the Runway*. See you next week!"

Fran calls it a wrap and Paige lets out an aggravated sigh then walks out of the room. After the door closes, I hear JJ and Alistair chuckling.

"You guys thought that was funny?" I ask them as I turn off my camera, sliding it down into my Birkin bag.

"A little bit." JJ makes a sheepish smile.

"Well, I doubt that Paige agrees with you." I zip my bag. "And now she's probably mad at me too."

"She'll get over it," Fran assures me.

Sure enough, as we ride back to the hotel, Paige is extra quiet and I can tell she's unhappy. I consider asking her about it, but then decide to just let her chill for awhile. When we get to the hotel, she's still giving us the silent treatment. Fran and I exchange glances and then just shrug.

"Anyone interested in dinner later?" Fran asks as we get out of the elevator.

"I'll do room service tonight," Paige tells her as she un-locks her door.

"I better check my phone messages," I say. "In case Blake made it into town. I'll let you know."

Fran just nods then goes to her room. As I go into my room, I feel guilty. Like maybe this is my fault that Paige is feeling hurt. It's a familiar feeling, a feeling that I've struggled with my whole life—whenever Paige threw a tantrum, I would give in and give her what she wanted. But is it really my job to make sure my sister is happy? Seriously, it's not like I had any control over André. And what about his runway comment to me? I could have hurt feelings over that too, but did Paige do anything to make me feel better? Suddenly I feel irritated at my sister. I shake my head and kick off my shoes as I check for phone messages, deciding to put the whole thing behind me. I'm partially relieved to learn that Blake and Benjamin won't make it to Paris until tomorrow.

I change into comfortable clothes, telling myself that I'm not going to obsess over my sister and her little hang ups. If she wants to have a pity party of one in Paris, she's more than welcome to it. But as soon as I make that decision, I start to feel guilty. What kind of sister am I anyway? Furthermore, what kind of a Christian am I? Where is my love and compassion?

I'm just about to go over and knock on her door when the landline phone in my room rings. Hoping it's Paige wanting to be friends again, I grab it up, but someone in a thick French accent tells me there is something for me to pick up from the concierge. I hurry down, thinking that maybe Blake has done something sweet like send me flowers or candy—and candy actually sounds good since I'm starving. But it turns out to be a large box. A very nice box with an envelope taped to the top of it with my name on it.

I take it up to my room and open the envelope and quickly read.

Dear Erin,
I know you love your sister. And I know your sister loves your Birkin bag. So here is a bag for you to give to her.
Sincerely,
Gabin

I tear open the tissue paper and there it is—a pale pink Birkin bag! I can't believe it—I go totally nuts, hugging the bag to my chest and hopping up and down like I just won the lottery. This is too good! I cannot wait. But first I calm myself down. With the bag behind my back, I quietly knock on Paige's door. When she opens the door, she is already in her pajamas, her hair is pulled into a sloppy bun, and she's got some kind of white paste all over her face, which makes her look kind of ghostly.

"I have a surprise for you," I tell her with a totally blank expression.

"Oh?" She waves me into her room. "First let me go wash this masque off before it turns to cement, okay?"

"Okay." I stand by her bathroom door, the bag still concealed behind my back.

"I wanted to say I'm sorry," she calls out as she splashes water on her face. "For the way I acted at Givenchy. It was really childish."

"That's okay," I tell her. "I understand."

She's drying her face. "I knew you'd understand, Erin. But I still need to say I'm sorry." She makes a sad little smile. "I mean, you're not just my sister, you're my best friend, and I hate it when I act like that. So, forgive me, okay?"

"Absolutely." Now I can't help myself; I'm grinning.

"What have you got?" she asks curiously.

"Oh, nothing much ..." I start to giggle.

"What?"

I hold out the pink Birkin bag and it looks like Paige's eyes are going to pop out. "No way," she says quietly.

I nod. "Uh-huh. *Way.*"

"No way!"

"Gabin sent it here for me to give to you, Paige."

She grabs the bag, acting exactly like I did just minutes ago. "It's perfect. It's wonderful. It's gorgeous!" She's parading in front of the mirror. "It even looks great with pajamas!" She comes over and hugs me. "Thanks, Erin! You are the best sister in the world."

I laugh. "Well, Gabin's the one you need to thank. We both do."

"Man, he really must have it bad for you, Erin." She looks at me with wide eyes. "I thought you said it was over."

I shrug. "There really wasn't anything to be over. I mean, we really were only friends."

Still hugging the bag, she sits down on her bed, patting the spot beside her. "We really need to talk, little sister. Between Benjamin and Dylan ... and Blake and Gabin ... you and I have some things to start sorting out and thinking through."

I sit down and consider this. I fully realize that Paige probably has a lot more sorting to do than me, but at the same time it's nice to be included. I nod. "Where do we begin?" I ask.

So here we sit, just two slightly confused sisters in Paris, talking about guys and life and even God, while we wait for room service to arrive with our dinner. And I think, *this is good—this is how it should be.* Although we still have a couple of things left to do in Paris, I think that the most important part of this trip is right here in this room. And I thank God for that.

ON THE RUNWAY

SPOTLIGHT

A Novel

Bestselling Author
**Melody
Carlson**

LONDON, ENGLAND

GREAT BRITAIN

Chapter
1

I never wanted to be famous. I know there are people, like my best friend Mollie, who probably don't believe me. Of course, that's because Mollie would absolutely love to be famous. Unfortunately, Mollie's acting career is on hold because her baby is due in about three months.

Since I *never* wanted to be a celebrity, I'm experiencing some real culture shock over what's happened since our show *On the Runway* became a real hit. According to our producer, Helen Hudson, we're one of the hottest reality TV shows running right now and sponsors are lining up. This is totally great news—and I am happy for my sister, Paige, because this is her dream. But I'm still not comfortable with all that comes with it.

My general dislike of the limelight is not because I'm some highly evolved Christian who is too holy and humble to want to hog all this attention. Paige's theory that my fame-phobia is a result of my poor self-image isn't exactly right either. In fact, I think my self-image is fairly normal. I mean, how many young women—or old women—look in the mirror and absolutely adore what they see? Well, besides Paige. But honestly, I'm pretty much okay with my looks. And most of the time, despite having a drop-dead gorgeous sibling, I'm thankful that God made me the way he did.

My discomfort with celebrity is basically selfish—I happen to like my normal life and I enjoy my privacy, and I'd rather fly beneath the radar of the paparazzi than be running from them.

I think being in Paris last month gave me a false sense of obscurity-security, because Paige and I were able to film our episodes and go about our daily lives with very little intrusion from the media. Of course, Paige was a little troubled by this.

"It's like no even one knows who we are," she said as we walked through the Charles de Gaulle International Airport unobserved.

"Or they just don't care," I teased. And, really, Paris is kind of like that—subdued and slightly aloof. I think Parisians, totally unlike Americans, aren't too interested in celebrity spotting.

But Paige seemed bummed. Her way to protest was to sport her newest pair of Gucci sunglasses, hold her chin high, and strut through the terminal like she was a real star. And I'll admit I noticed heads turn. I'm not sure they knew who she was, or cared, though: she is simply an eye-catcher.

Fortunately, for Paige, we were spotted and even photographed when we arrived at LAX the next day. By then I had on sunglasses too, but mine were to hide the dark circles beneath my eyes after a mostly sleepless night during the eleven-hour flight.

"Is it true that you and Benjamin Kross were vacationing

together in France?" a reporter from one of the gossip shows asked Paige as we waited to spot our luggage in baggage claim.

Paige smiled and tossed her head. "We were with a number of interesting people in France," she said brightly. "Benjamin was there for a few days as well."

"What did you think about Benjamin's settlement with Mia Renwick's family?" the reporter persisted.

"I think it's really none of my business." Paige smiled.

"What about rumors that you and Dylan Marceau are engaged?" the other reporter asked next.

Paige laughed. "They are just that—rumors."

"But are you involved with Dylan Mar—"

"I think Dylan is a brilliant designer and he's a good friend."

Just then I spotted some of our luggage on the carousel, and I abandoned my sister to her adoring paparazzi in order to help our director, Fran, drag the bags off. Sure, we might be "famous," but we still carry our own bags. At least most of the time, anyway. Blake has reminded me more than once that his offer to carry my bags, do shoulder rubs and pedicures, run errands, take out the trash—or whatever—is still good if the show wants to take him along with us. So far I don't think the show is too interested in Blake.

Unfortunately, Blake's interest in the show doesn't seem to be going away. And way too often, despite me asking him not to, he wants to talk about it. So why am I surprised when he starts in after our fellowship group? Several of us, including Lionel, Sonya, and Mollie, decided to extend the evening by meeting at Starbucks for coffee, and I've just taken a sip of my mocha when Blake brings it up.

"Did you guys hear that Erin is going to London next month?" he announces.

"Yeah, and she's not even excited about it." Mollie rolls her eyes at me.

"It's not that I'm *not* excited," I protest. "It's just that we haven't been back from Paris for that long. And we're trying to plan my mom's wedding and—"

"Excuses, excuses . . ." Mollie waves her hand. "You are off living the life and all you do is complain, complain."

I frown at her. "Really? Do I complain that much?"

She gives me a sheepish smile. "Well, I might exaggerate a bit. It's only because I'm jealous. I would so love to go to London."

"Me too," Blake chimes in.

Mollie makes a face at Blake. "But you already got to go with Erin to Paris, so if anyone gets to go to London with her, it should be me."

"FYI," I remind her, "Blake went to France with *Benjamin Kross*, not me." And, okay, I know I'm doing this as much for Lionel's sake as for Mollie's, since he already questioned why Blake made that trip. I'm not sure if he was jealous or merely curious, but it's a topic I try to avoid.

Things have been a little awkward with both guys since I returned from the trip and put the brakes on both relationships. As soon as I got home from Paris, I called both Blake and Lionel and told them the same thing: that Paige and I had made a pact not to date for a while and to focus on the show.

"Yeah, Erin didn't actually invite me." Blake turns to Lionel, almost like he's trying to get a reaction. "And when I got to Bordeaux, she already had a French boyfriend."

"You know that Gabin was *not* a boyfriend." I shake my

finger at Blake. "He's just a good friend." We'd been over this several times already.

"Yeah, but he gave you that great bag." Mollie points to my black Birkin bag, which has kind of become my signature piece of late. Not because it's such a fashion statement as much as it's really great for carrying my camera and junk.

"So what are you going to be covering in London?" Lionel asks me.

"Isn't it Fashion Week there?" Mollie asks.

"Actually Fashion Week London isn't until September," I explain. "And the show will probably send us back to London then. This trip is to coincide with a new British TV show. It's kind of like *America's Next Top Model*. Paige is going to be a judge and we'll use that for an episode, then we'll do some episodes on the Brit fashion scene. And we'll stay at the May Fair and—"

"The May Fair is like the swankiest hotel in the coolest fashion district in London," Mollie explains. "I looked it up on the Internet and I was pea green with envy."

"And you're not excited about that?" Sonya asks me. She's been the quiet person in the group tonight. As usual, I wonder if she's still feeling a little out of sorts because of her breakup with Blake. And because she might secretly blame me for losing him, although I'd beg to differ. Sometimes I catch these glances from her and, despite Blake's assurance, I suspect Sonya isn't totally over him.

"It's not that I'm *not* excited," I say for the second time. Like is anyone listening. "It's just that—"

"Oh, admit it," Mollie pushes in. "You're like the heel-dragging, reluctant little starlet. Your TV show is handed to you on a silver platter and you turn your nose up and—"

"It was *not* handed to me," I protest. "It's Paige's show. I'm just a secondary character, if that. I'm the lowly camera girl and—"

"Not true," Blake interrupts. "That makeover episode in Paris sent your popularity soaring."

I frown at him. "And how do you know that?"

He grins. "Because I pay attention to these things."

"So do I," Mollie tells me. "And, whether you like it or not, that episode turned you into a star. So get over it."

Okay, now I don't have a response.

"I think they're right," Lionel confirms. "I saw that episode too, and I'm guessing that your role in the show is going to change."

"*Is* changing," Mollie interjects.

"And you're not happy about that?" Sonya looks like she'd love to slap me.

"It's just not what I wanted," I try to explain. "It's Paige's gig, not mine."

"Did you even listen to Eric's message tonight?" Blake demands with a twinkle in his eye.

I consider this. Eric is an assistant pastor at our church and he led the fellowship group tonight. But at the moment I'm blank. "I listened," I tell him. "But I'm having a hard time remembering . . ."

"Eric said that God sometimes puts us in bad situations for good reasons." Mollie grins at me like she thinks I'll give her a gold star.

"Oh, yeah." I nod. "Thanks, Mollie."

"Like Joseph," Lionel reiterates. "Sold as a slave by his brothers, then falsely accused and put in prison—talk about some hard situations."

"But God had a plan," Blake adds. "He worked it together for good."

I nod, knowing where this is going. "You guys are right. I do have the wrong attitude about the show."

"You need to see your TV show as an opportunity," Blake tells me. "You can be a light in a dark place, Erin. Remember that night in Bordeaux."

"What night in Bordeaux?" Lionel asks with a creased brow.

"It's like everyone was starting to get into a big fight," I explain. "Our hostess was having some issues. Paige was caught in the middle. Yet somehow Blake managed to get everyone gathered around a campfire and we sang and stuff, and then, before the evening ended, Blake actually gave his testimony and it was pretty cool."

Lionel actually gives Blake a fist bump. "That is very cool. Way to go, Blake."

Blake smiles and I can tell he appreciates this coming from Lionel. I must admit it's a relief to see a couple of Christian guys acting more like brothers than competitors.

"So maybe you need to remember Joseph next time you feel like complaining," Mollie tells me. "He didn't exactly like being sold as a slave or doing time, but he did his best and God used him in some big ways."

"And the bigger your role on your show becomes, the more visible you'll be," Lionel says. "And the more influence you'll have ..."

"To be a light in a dark place," Blake finishes.

And so that's my new attitude—or it's what I'm trying to adopt as my new attitude. I obviously need God's help to carry it off. But my goal now is to do my best job, and even if I don't particularly love being on the show, I'll give it my all and just see what happens. I thought that would make everyone happy—especially everyone working on the show.

Unfortunately, I quickly discover that might not be the case. The following week, after previewing a couple of the Paris episodes, Paige and I are in a planning meeting with Helen and Fran and the rest of the crew when Helen suggests that my role in the show has changed.

"I know that you like filming the show," she tells me. "But I see the show going a different direction now. We no longer need a camera girl."

"What do you mean?" Paige demands. "You can't take Erin off the show. I need her!"

Helen laughs. "No, of course we're not taking her off the show. *On the Runway* needs her too, Paige."

Paige has a relieved smile. "Oh, you scared me."

"Sorry." Helen pats her hand. "What I'm saying is that Erin needs to become more of a partner now."

Paige's forehead creases ever so slightly. "A partner?"

"Yes. No more remaining behind the scenes. The fans are connecting with Erin in a big way now. She needs to come out of the background and become a featured costar."

"A featured costar?" Paige looks unconvinced.

"Of course, you'll still be the host," Helen assures her. "But Erin will play a more significant and visible role alongside of you."

"How, exactly?" Paige glances at me then back to Helen.

"Mostly by being herself." Helen smiles at me like I should get this. But frankly, I don't.

"We want Erin to bring her opinions about fashion onto the screen," Fran injects. "You two girls are so different. Sometimes it's hard to believe you're really sisters." She laughs. "But it's apparent that our fans are diverse as well. And we've gotten some great viewer responses in regard to topics like green design and economical fashion."

"So we've decided we need to include more segments along these lines," Helen finishes for her. "And Erin is the perfect one to take us there."

Everything in me wants to stand up and protest—to remind everyone in this room of our original agreement, that I am merely "Camera Girl" and that it's acceptable for me to remain a wallflower. But at the same time I remember the conversation at Starbucks on Saturday night. I remember how my friends challenged me to change my attitude and let God use me however he wants in regard to the show. So how do I back down now?

Paige lets out a little laugh then shakes her head. "Okay, I'll admit that *sounds* like a sensible plan and, naturally, we want to expand our audience. But there's one itty-bitty problem."

"What's that?" Helen adjusts her glasses and peers at Paige.

Paige makes what feels like a patronizing smile at me. "We all know how stubborn my little sister can be. Of course, Erin would never agree to this, *would you, Erin?*"

Now all eyes are on me, and with a furrowed brow Helen points her silver pen in my direction. "Is that right, Erin? Are you still going to play the spoiler?"

I clear my throat, which suddenly feels like sandpaper.

"Speak up," Helen urges.

"Actually ..." I glance at Paige then back at Helen. "I am actually ... sort of ... open."

Paige's jaw drops ever so slightly. "Open? Open to what?"

"Open to ... you know ... whatever. I mean, if the show needs me to step up, well, I'm willing."

Helen clasps her hands together. "I just knew you'd be game, Erin. I felt it in my bones. When I saw the initial footage from Paris I said to myself, our little Erin is finally growing up!"

Suddenly they're all talking and making plans, and it's obvious that they've already given this some serious thought, but when I glance over at Paige, who is sitting silently, I can tell she's not really on board. And the way she's looking is reminiscent of something ... something I'd nearly forgotten ... something that happened a long time ago.

When we were little—I was in kindergarten and Paige was in first grade—my sister begged my parents for gymnastic classes. Her friend Kelsey was bragging about how she was going to become an Olympic gymnast (which never happened), so Paige insisted she needed lessons too. My parents eventually agreed, but Dad decided both Paige and I should be enrolled in the academy so that I wouldn't feel left out. Naturally, I was happy to be included since I already loved jumping, climbing, and rolling around like a monkey. But after a couple of months at the academy, which I thoroughly enjoyed, Paige's interest started waning until she refused to go at all.

Years later, I learned by accident that Paige's reason for quitting gymnastics was simply because I'd been outshining her and she did not like to be second best at anything. Although I continued going for a while, it wasn't long before my sister convinced me that gymnastics was silly and the outfits we had to wear were even worse, and that it would be much more fun to take dance classes instead. Naturally, she turned out to be far more gifted and graceful at ballet than me. And, once again, she was back in her comfort zone—where she reigned.

Although my sister has grown up some since then—she's matured a lot these past few months, and our relationship is stronger than ever—I still suspect that some of her old habits die hard. Forcing Paige to share the limelight with me could come with its own set of challenges. Which brings to mind Joseph ... and how his own brothers sold him to strangers. Okay, I'm pretty sure my sister wouldn't sink quite that low. But it does give me pause to wonder.

On the Runway Series
from Melody Carlson

When Paige and Erin Forrester are offered their own TV show, sisterly bonds are tested as the girls learn that it takes two to keep their once-in-a-lifetime project afloat.

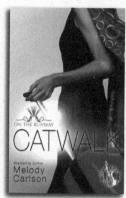

Premiere
Book One

Catwalk
Book Two

Rendezvous
Book Three

Spotlight
Book Four

Glamour
Book Five

Ciao
Book Six

Available in stores and online!

ZONDERVAN®
.com

Carter House Girls Series
from Melody Carlson

Mix six teenage girls and one '60s fashion icon (retired, of course) in an old Victorian-era boarding home. Add boys and dating, a little high school angst, and throw in a Kate Spade bag or two ... and you've got the Carter House Girls, Melody Carlson's new chick lit series for young adults!

Mixed Bags
Book One

Stealing Bradford
Book Two

Homecoming Queen
Book Three

Viva Vermont!
Book Four

Lost in Las Vegas
Book Five

New York Debut
Book Six

Spring Breakdown
Book Seven

Last Dance
Book Eight

Available in stores and online!